Monsters, despite their most vile
reputations, can still be used for good.
So long as someone shows them the light.

-Dimitri Darksmith

BE SCARY!
2016

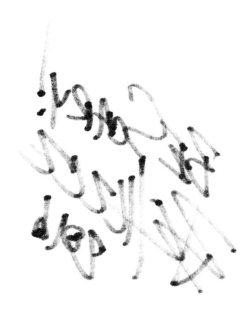

FEAR & SUNSHINE

BOOK TWO OF THE DARKSMITH FAMILY LEGACY

Written & Illustrated by
Donovan Scherer

Fear & Sunshine

Text & Illustrations Copyright © 2009 by Donovan Scherer

Published in 2009 by Ratatat Graphics LLC

For information regarding permission, write to:

Ratatat Graphics LLC
5605 Sheridan Rd., #1172
Kenosha, WI 53141-1172

ISBN: 978-0-9841746-1-4
Library of Congress Control Number: 2009913592

www.fearandsunshine.com
www.donovanscherer.com

For my Family and Friends

Thank you for all the
inspiration and support

Special Thanks to:

Javi Vega, Jeanne Scherer, Dan Merfeld,
Doug Scherer, Svend Widvey,
Chad Tuura, Kelli Cross

Fear & Sunshine

Contents

Introduction

Since the closure of Darksmith Manor and death of its Duke, Dominick, the creatures forged there are at a loss. Over the course of the last seven years, without his guiding hand, they have been lost in a world in which they have no place. They roam aimlessly or remain hidden away, waiting for a new path to follow.

Unfortunately, as his efforts to gain entry into the sealed Darksmith Manor have failed time and time again, the fiend known as Fear is now determined to usher in a dark new dawn. With no hope of stealing the power of Darksmith, he turns his evil toward both the monsters left to fend for themselves and any unlucky innocents in his way.

If anyone can defeat Fear, the young heiress of Darksmith Manor might embody her fragile world's last hope.

- Death -

Chapter One

Death in the Family

ONE BY ONE, eight tiny feet shuffled along until, finally, the little creature reached the goal of his journey and rested atop the peak of the sleeping giant. Then, to his horror, the vast plains which he had just ventured across began to move. Soon, two eyes fixed their gaze upon him.

Eight tiny feet, their owner too afraid to move, kept the little spider locked in place as the giant's hand moved slowly toward him. Surprisingly, the finger gave only the slightest nudge as it scooped him up, and the spider rode this chariot to the edge of the world he had known. Just as gently as it had picked him up, the finger placed him on the edge of the giant's hammock.

He could see the dawn sun break through the drooping trees of Wandering Willows and bounce back up off the small creek coursing beyond the garden. The spider

looked up, thankfully, to his new friend, the giant, as she picked up a stuffed rabbit from her floor and left the bedroom to join her family for breakfast.

The girl shambled down the hall to find a man and woman already preparing breakfast. The kitchen had no break between it and the living room aside from a table plopped in the center. The handmade furniture strewn about the room gave it the appearance of an oversized tree house, which was exactly what it was.

"Good morning, Sunshine!" the man smiled, far too cheerily for this early in the day. "Come give me a hand with the juice. I've finally got this thing up and running."

Sunshine pushed a chair beside him and climbed up. Grabbing the bag of green apples, she began handing them to him. He stuffed them into the crude device made out of a hollowed out log with a crank attached to its side.

Ever since Sunshine was old enough to ask about the medallion she wore around her neck, she had known that the Salientes weren't her birth parents. Despite that, she had always loved them as if they were. Pop, with his constant ingenuity and innovation, which had led them to a perfectly content life outside the hustle-bustle of the towns surrounding Wandering Willows, and Momsy, with the patience to put up with it, had become her true family. Regardless of the happiness she had with her life as it was, there seemed to be an itch forming in the back of her mind. A subconscious unsettling feeling had recently begun to visit her while she slept.

"I had another dream about my real parents, I think," Sunshine told Pop and Momsy. "I still couldn't see their faces, but I'm pretty sure it's them."

Pop set down his glass of juice. "Well, Sunshine. It is your dream, so if you think it's them, I'm sure it is." He turned to his wife, "Maybe your sister could hunt down a picture of them. What do you think?"

Momsy thought about it for a moment. "I suppose she could. It has been some time since your Aunt Constance came for a visit, hasn't it?"

Sunshine's eyes sparkled at the thought of her aunt. She had always been intrigued by Constance Adora, Momsy's younger, yellow-eyed sister who always carried a scent of campfire and pine needles.

"Well," said Momsy, regarding the eagerness that now washed over Sunshine's face, "I'll write her a letter today to invite her over."

Sunshine trotted along a tree-lined path, her stuffed rabbit in hand. "Oh, Bunny, I can't wait for Auntie Constance to come visit. I hope she can find a picture of my parents, too. But that's okay if she can't. We have the best adventures when she's here."

Sunshine stopped in her tracks and pulled Bunny up to her face. "You know what we should do? We should practice! We should go on a practice adventure, so that when Auntie Constance gets here, she'll be like, 'Oooo, wow, you guys are so good at adventuring,' and then she'll come on one of our adventures, and we can be the guides!"

Sunshine stared at Bunny, grinning from ear to ear. Bunny stared back, expressing as much excitement as possible for a stuffed rabbit. Sunshine squinted happily at her inanimate little friend. "I know just the place to take her."

Two long ears slowly crept over the surface of the well. Soon after, those two long ears were followed by two button eyes. Then, those two long ears and two button eyes were joined by the face of a little girl, hidden beneath an orange headband and mud smeared on her nose and cheeks to resemble war paint. "There's got to be some treasure down there," Sunshine whispered to Bunny.

Bunny stared blankly back at her. Sunshine smiled cheerfully, "You're a brave one, little guy."

Inch by inch, the bucket carrying Bunny dropped lower

into the well. "Do you see anything?" Sunshine yelled down.

No response. "Okay, maybe a little lower." Sunshine gave the bucket more and more line until she heard it hit the surface of the water.

"Do you see anything?" she repeated.

No response. "Okay," she yelled. "We'll come back tomorrow with a snorkel."

She raised the bucket back to the top of the well and pulled out her stuffed rabbit. "I think we might need more practice adventuring before we can invite Auntie Constance along."

Sunshine skipped down the dirt road, Bunny sitting on her shoulders. "Maybe we need a treasure map, or somebody to save, or a monster to capture before we can go on an adventure." Sunshine wandered over to a stump by the side of the road and sat down on it, putting Bunny in her lap. She tousled his ears.

"Maybe we're not just supposed to go on an adventure," she said to Bunny, sadly. "Maybe adventure is just supposed to find …"

Sunshine stopped speaking as she noticed a man on the other side of the road. He was wearing a dark cloak

and resting against a tree. Sunshine stood up, clutching
Bunny tightly, and walked closer to the stranger. Although
Sunshine had always been told not to talk to strangers,
it was the first time she had ever actually seen one in
Wandering Willows, and curiosity took hold.

As Sunshine moved closer and closer, she still wasn't able
to see the stranger's face beneath his strange, dark cloak.
The cloak itself intrigued Sunshine. It was dark, but
black didn't quite seem to be the right name for the color.
Although the stranger was sitting in the shade, the noon
sun was plenty bright enough for her to see him. The
cloak seemed to have no color, like it was empty, not really
even there.

A bit confused, but still wanting to see who he was,
Sunshine continued forward. "Hello?" she said, not sure
whether or not to even expect a response. Closer yet she
moved. "Hello?"

She was now in front of the stranger. "Hey, mister – "
Sunshine stopped as a breeze caught hold of the hood
that covered the man's face.

She saw that there wasn't a face at all. Instead, she gaped
at a skull surrounded by the darkness of the colorless
cloak. Sunshine let out a tiny gasp as she squeezed Bunny.

Then, as she slowly stepped back, the skull turned up to
face her. "Hello, Sunshine Saliente."

Sunshine let out a scream as the cloaked figure rose
from the ground with the help of a staff fixed with a
long, curved blade. She looked Bunny in the face, who
responded with his typical blank response. She then
looked back at the skull-faced stranger who had begun
to approach her. Hoping for advice on what to do now,
Sunshine looked back at Bunny. Not getting any help,
she screamed and burst into a sprint down the dirt road
toward home.

The door flew open as Sunshine crashed through,
colliding with the table where the family had eaten their
breakfast, and knocking over the remaining juice. Without
any hesitation, she whipped Bunny across the room into a
laundry basket, which flipped over him and hid the rabbit
out of sight. Sunshine scurried back to the door, slamming
the bolt shut.

"Sunshine!" Pop shouted as he rushed into the room.
"What's going on?" Sunshine ran to him and scrambled
up his back until she clutched his head while perched on
his shoulders.

Momsy came in and hurried over to them. "Sunshine,
what's wrong?" she asked, trying to comfort the child.

Then, at the door ... knock, knock, knock.

After peeling her off his head, Pop put Sunshine into
Momsy's arms and quietly crept over to the window to

peek out and see what their girl was running from.

Somewhat baffled, he looked back at Sunshine and then smiled. "It's okay," he whispered. "There's no reason to be scared." Sunshine jumped down and hid behind Momsy's leg as Pop began unlocking the door. Sunshine closed her eyes. Why would her parents do this?

"Hi, Flora. Hi, Salvo" The voice didn't seem to fit a cloak-wearing skeleton. "Hey, kiddo, what are you up to?" It wasn't until the scent of campfire and pine needles hit her nose that Sunshine was ready to open her eyes.

"Auntie Constance!" Sunshine squealed as she leapt into the young woman's arms, forcing her into a spin. Sunshine quickly grabbed the overly wide brim of Constance's hat, "Hurry! We have to hide. There's a monster out there!"

Constance let out an amused chuckle as she set Sunshine down. "It's okay," she said as she straightened Sunshine's orange headband. "He's with me."

Sunshine's face was fixed upon the doorway as the tall, dark-cloaked figure stood behind her aunt.

Sitting in a chair much too big for her, Sunshine stared across the handmade coffee table, baffled yet suspicious about the unusual stranger who sat across from her.

"So," Pop said as he paced behind Sunshine. "This is Death."

Sunshine flinched and looked up to her dear Auntie Constance, who sat next to Death on the small couch. "Really?" she squeaked.

"The one and only," Constance said while smiling all too comfortably, in Sunshine's opinion, for a person seated next to Death.

"Well, sir. I do believe we owe you a long overdue thank you," Pop said heartily. Sunshine's jaw dropped.

As Pop patted Sunshine on the head and gave her a grin, Momsy sat down next to her. "You see, Sunshine," she started, getting the girl's attention. "Our guest here helped bring you to us when you were just a baby. He even knew your real parents when they were alive."

Sunshine looked at Death and for the first time since meeting him, considered the possibility that maybe he wasn't a monster.

"It is because of that," Death stated as he stood from the couch, "that we are here today. Sunshine, do you still have the medallion that your mother left for you?"

Sunshine scooted back in her chair and then reached into her shirt, pulling out the medallion with the skull-shaped emblem and metallic, golden sunrays.

"Good, my child, good. Although it may seem only a trinket, within that heirloom lies the key to your birthright, the path to your destiny. You, Sunshine Saliente are the heiress to Darksmith Manor!" As Death burst into gruff laughter, darkness seemed to fill the afternoon sky.

"Ahem," Constance interrupted. "I asked you not to do that."

Death looked at her, somewhat embarrassed as the day returned to its normal brightness. "Come on, Constance. How often do I get to do stuff like this?" Sunshine looked back and forth between the two as they argued about theatrics. Then Constance knelt down beside her.

"Let's go for a walk."

Sunshine and Constance made their way beyond the family's garden behind the house and walked along the small creek. Taking a seat on a bench beside the stream, Sunshine set Bunny in her lap and looked up to Constance. "Momsy was going to invite you to come visit today. Did you know, and that's why you came? I've been practicing adventuring and even Bunny comes along. We haven't found any treasure or anything yet, but we think we just need more practice."

Constance laughed, "Good, I'm glad you've been practicing. I actually have a big adventure I need you to go on." Constance paused as a look of melancholy came over her.

Sunshine crawled up onto Constance's lap. "What's a Darksmith Manor?"

Constance leaned back a bit and gave Sunshine a little smile. "Darksmith Manor," Constance said, "is where your real parents used to live. After your father, Dominick Darksmith, sent you to live here, he locked up Darksmith Manor, and nobody's been there ever since."

Sunshine scrunched her nose, looking slightly puzzled. "Why did he lock it up?"

"Well," Constance answered hesitantly. "When you were just a baby, there was a bad, bad man named Fear. He wanted to take you away. Then, he could have been in charge of Darksmith Manor. When your father locked up Darksmith Manor, Fear thought you were still inside, so that way, he wouldn't go looking for you."

Tears started to fill Sunshine's eyes. "Is … is Mr. Fear still looking for me?"

Constance looked woefully at the little girl and caressed her hair. "No, he isn't."

Sunshine, now confused, wiped her eyes. "Then, what's wrong? If he's not looking for me, then it's okay, right?"

"No, Sunshine," Constance said firmly. "It's not okay. Now that Fear has stopped trying to find you, there's nothing to keep him from focusing all of the evil inside him elsewhere. He's terrorizing people, burning down whole towns. He's leading an army of …" Constance stopped, afraid she had already said enough to give the girl nightmares. "Sunshine, what Death said inside, about your destiny and your being the heiress of Darksmith Manor … The only way to stop Fear is for you to take back the manor. You will be safe there. I'll make sure of that. There are a lot of people counting on your coming back, Sunshine."

Constance took Sunshine's hand and began walking back toward the house. Sunshine looked down at Bunny. "I'm scared. If Mr. Fear finds out I'm there, he might try to get me. I can't let him hurt anybody. As long as you're with me, I think I'll be okay." Sunshine looked at Bunny and then up to Constance. "I'll do it."

When they returned to the house, Momsy ran up to Sunshine, eyes red with tears. Still holding Bunny, Sunshine flung both her arms around her foster mother as she was picked up into the air.

Pop walked over to Constance. "You told her then, right?" Constance nodded. Pop leaned in closer. "Did you explain to her exactly what Darksmith Manor does?"

Constance shook her head. "There's only so much that a little girl should be asked of in one day. Death told you ... we have to leave before dawn to catch the boat."

Pop frowned as he nodded. Constance left the room with Death, while Pop joined his wife and Sunshine.

Sunshine looked up to him. "You're not coming with, are you?"

Pop put his hand on her shoulder, "No, Sunshine. We can't, not yet."

Momsy carried Sunshine to her room, Pop following behind. As they lifted Sunshine into her hammock, they each leaned in to give her one last good night kiss. Sunshine wearily looked up at them, "Why am I going to bed so early? The sun hasn't even gone down yet."

Momsy kneeled beside her. "You'll be leaving very early, before the sun comes up. You have a long way to go, and we need to get your things ready. It's quite a journey you have ahead of yourself. No matter how things are there, just remember that your Pop and I are thinking of you."

Sunshine smiled a tired smile and closed her eyes.

Chapter Two

Beyond the Willows

One by one, eight tiny feet shuffled along until, once again, they had found their place high atop the peak of the sleeping giant. One at a time, each tiny foot tapped down to wake the giant from its slumber, and one at a time, each of the giant's eyes slowly opened to gaze upon the miniscule little creature.

"Hello again, little friend," Sunshine greeted the spider.

The spider hopped down from the girl's nose and scurried along the hammock. She squinted to watch the spider until noticing something moving in the darkness. Sunshine sat up and rubbed her eyes in disbelief as her purple and orange shirt floated gently in front of her. Then, at the edge of her hammock, she saw her little friend as it jumped onto the hovering garment. Sunshine crawled closer to her shirt, and as she did, she began to see a faint

light bouncing off the silky webs that held her clothing.

"You got my clothes ready?" she asked the spider, amazed. "Thank you very much."

Sunshine and Bunny arrived downstairs to find everyone finalizing preparations for the journey.

"Oh, goody," Momsy smiled. "You're already awake."

Sunshine, still rubbing some of the sleep out of her eyes, dragged her feet across the floor. "Good morning, everyone."

Momsy knelt down in front of Sunshine and wrapped a jacket around her shoulders. "Now, Sunshine. I have a very special gift for you to take along on your journey."

Sunshine watched as Momsy pulled out an odd-looking flower with big, floppy, blue petals.

"It's a flower?" Sunshine acknowledged, not sure what to make of it. "It's a nice flower, but it looks kind of weird."

Momsy smiled and pulled off the bottom of the stem. "It's a pen. I've had this for as long as I can remember, and it's never run dry. I want you to have it so that you can write us letters and draw pictures to send to us. You can chronicle all of your adventures at Darksmith Manor for us to read about."

Sunshine smiled as she took the pen. "I will." She then looked up at the parents she had known all of her life and was overcome with grief. She dropped Bunny as she threw her arms around them.

As Sunshine and the Salientes walked outside, they found Constance waiting in front of the house. Constance picked up a small bag and smiled at Sunshine. "Alright, kiddo. Are you ready to go?"

Sunshine looked around. "Where's the rest of my stuff?"

"Right here," Death grunted as he lugged a trunk through the front door. "Stand back, everyone," he ordered. Lifting the trunk onto his shoulder with one hand, Death raised his scythe with the other. "I'll meet you on the other side." As the bottom of Death's scythe struck the ground, smoke swirled up and engulfed him. Once it had cleared, Death was gone.

Sunshine's eyes lit up. "Can we do that?"

"Sorry, kiddo," Constance said. "We have to travel the old-fashioned way."

Constance looked up at the cloud-covered night sky as they made their way down the long dirt road. "It's really too bad the sky isn't clear. There's a full moon tonight."

Sunshine slowed down a bit to walk beside Constance.

"You know what?" Sunshine asked her. "People say monsters come out when there's a full moon. Do you want to know what I think? I think if monsters come out with the full moon, then it's easier for people to see where they're going. Then, they can run away easier."

Constance's yellow eyes twinkled in the moonlight, "What do you know about monsters?"

Sunshine shrugged, "I don't know. I never really believed in monsters. Shadows in my room never scared me. I always got along with creepy critters. I used to have a pet bat, but I let him go. I don't think he liked being in a cage too much. I don't know ... I never met somebody with a skull for a face until yesterday. He's kind of funny, not like I'd think a monster would be. I like him. Death, hehe. I don't think I'd like that Mr. Fear, though. He sounds like a real meanie."

"Well," Constance said, watching the clouds drift across the sky. "Sunshine, assuming monsters are real, wouldn't you think that some could be good and some could

be bad? Just because somebody's a monster doesn't necessarily make them evil like Mr. Fear. He just happens to be an evil monster."

Sunshine, beginning to get confused by the line of reasoning, wrinkled her nose at her aunt. "I guess, but who ever heard of a nice monster?"

Constance knelt down and handed her bag to Sunshine. Constance grinned at her. "You think I'm nice, don't you?"

The clouds parted, revealing the full moon. As the lunar light shined down on them, Sunshine stepped back in terror. Constance's yellow eyes glowed bright as she fell to her hands. The fabric of her tan dress seemed to grow into long strands of hair while coppery-colored fur jetted out from her skin. Sunshine watched claws sprout from the paws that were once the hands of her dear aunt. As the young woman's face came to resemble that of a wolf, she faced the moon, letting out a howl. Sunshine, gripping Bunny tighter than she ever had, looked into the yellow eyes of the beast and, somehow, saw her aunt inside. "Auntie Constance?" the little girl's voice trembled.

The wolf lurked toward Sunshine and leaned in inches from her face. She couldn't hold in the giggle as the canine tongue licked her cheek. "Hop on," the wolf growled playfully.

Holding on to the floppy hat strapped around the wolf's neck, Sunshine cheered in delight as they sped through the countryside in a furry blur. She had never been this far from home and watched as the mountains of Shwibala passed by far to the south. For some reason, the feel of the gallop through the grass and the sound of the wind blowing through her aunt's fur were oddly familiar. After what couldn't have been long enough for a full night, light began to dimly fill the sky, and the full moon faded beyond the edge of the world. Sunshine crawled down from Constance's back and sat in the grass to watch her regain her human form.

Spinning in a circle, Sunshine yipped, "That was so cool! Constance Adora. Aunt by day. Werewolf lady by night!"

Constance smiled. "Neat, huh? It comes with some trouble, but it's worth it."

"What kind of trouble?" Sunshine asked. Before she could get an answer, the girls reached the top of the hill.

Constance stopped walking. "There it is."

At the bottom of the hill, Sunshine saw a small seaside town. "Darksmith Manor is here?" Sunshine asked.

"No, no," Constance replied. "But there's our ride."

Beyond the Willows

Sunshine looked to where Constance pointed and saw a
small ship that looked as though it had floated up from the
bottom of the sea. "It looks like a ghost ship," Sunshine
whispered.

Constance grinned at her. "It is. Now, how about we go
get some breakfast?"

Sunshine and Constance made their way down to the
town as the ocean air filled their noses. Traders and
shoppers elbowed their way through the little markets
lined with tables of vendors selling whatever the sea
provided. Constance lifted Sunshine up and put her on
her shoulders. Sunshine did the same with Bunny.

Leaning down to Constance's ear, Sunshine asked,
"Where are all the cars and things? I thought towns had
big, crazy techno-loogies and stuff. Are these people like
Pop and Momsy?"

Constance laughed, "Kind of. Salvo and Flora, Pop and
Momsy, always just wanted to be able to take care of
themselves, to stay out of the big cities. For the people in
this town, it's their job to keep to themselves and to keep
the outside world out. And, of course, to keep the inside
world in."

The two entered a small inn and were seated at a booth

beside a huge, grimy window. Sunshine looked to
Constance. "Keep the inside world in?"

"Well," Constance said. "There's this place, Shwibala,
Wandering Willows and all, where things are how they are
and how you've always known them to be. Then, there's
where Darksmith Manor is, where things are what they
are which isn't necessarily how they are here ... Yeah, I
think that explains it."

Sunshine stared blankly at her aunt.

A young waiter with greasy hair and a twitchy eye arrived
at their table. "Welcome to the Typhoon Tavern, home
of Captain Moby's Seaweed Slammer. Today, we have a
special on boiled eel with a side of deep-fried pickled eggs.
Can I ... May I get you something to drink?"

"A glass of milk," Constance requested.

"Same for me, thank you," Sunshine said, squinty-eyed
and smiling at the nervous waiter.

"Okay. Back to what I was saying," Constance said as the
waiter backed into a neighboring table. "Most people and
things don't get to go back and forth. I get to because I'm
from here originally, and Death gets to because, well, he
gets to go any place he pleases. You, Sunshine, get to go
to the other side because that's where you're from anyway.
You're following this, right?"

"Nope," Sunshine replied.

"It's okay," Constance told her, "It'll make sense soon."

Sunshine twirled her flower pen between her fingers, trying to unravel what she had just heard. "Soooo, the place we're going to is a secret place?"

"Kind of. Most people do know about it but don't know they know about it. It's almost like a storybook place, but people don't realize it's a real place." With that, the waiter returned with two tall glasses of milk.

"Two Seaweed Slammers, please," Constance told him.

"I'm confused," Sunshine said, staring into her glass of milk as she continued to fiddle with her pen.

The waiter looked confused, "Don't be, it's delicious."

After their meal, the girls headed to the docks, passing various odd-looking people carrying various odd-looking things.

"Is it safe?" Sunshine whispered to Constance when they arrived at their boat. The boat appeared to be missing pieces that might be important to keep it afloat. The only part of the vessel that seemed to be in decent upkeep was the freshly painted name along its side, 'The Typhoonicane.'

"Of course it is," Constance smiled to Sunshine. "Captain Moby is the best sea captain around. He used to work for your father and before that, your grandfather."

"Really?" Sunshine said, looking surprised. "What did he do for them?"

Constance watched as a bushy-bearded, eye-patched sailor hustled along the deck of the ship and waved down at them. "He caught sea monsters, of course."

"Constance Adora," the bearded man shouted. "And this must be Sunshine. Come, come, and we'll set off." Sunshine followed Constance up the plank to the ship.

"Captain Moby, it's good to see you again."

"Aye, good to see you as well. Last we spoke, you were just a pup. And you, little Miss Darksmith, what a pleasure it is to meet you. Hope all's well with Salvo and your ma." Sunshine flinched as his one bloodshot eye twitched back and forth, examining her.

"Um, it's nice to meet you, Captain Moby. I had your Seaweed Slammer. It was very tasty."

"Ha!" Captain Moby burst out. "That plate's been doing

me wonders since I bought that old tavern."

Constance looked baffled, "You own the tavern?"

"Oh, ya. Ever since the untimely loss of young Sunshine's dear old Duke, business in my line of work has all but dried up. Had to see what else I could try my hand at. Fortunately, creatures of the deep can make for good eating, s'long as you cook 'em right. You try making it to the shop in Munstro in the fall when the krakens are in season. You'll never have anything that tastes as good as that."

"We'll do that," Constance said, forcing a grin as she tried to restrain herself from cringing at the memories of the last time she had the tentacled treat.

"Alright now," Captain Moby said, standing straight up in full captain pose. "Let's show you your quarters and head out to the high seas."

Sunshine and Constance stowed their belongings in their small, but cozy, room and headed back to the deck. As the Typhoonicane sailed off to unknown lands, Sunshine could see Wandering Willows, far to the west of the seaside town, vanish in the distance.

The creaking ship and rocking sea woke Sunshine up

from the small cot provided by Captain Moby. She crept over to her sleeping aunt and watched her nose, arms, and legs twitch. It looked like she dreamt of chasing rabbits through a field. Sunshine giggled about it as she wandered over to the ladder that led to the deck of the Typhoonicane. She made her way up to the deck and gazed in awe as the moonlight sparkled against the endless surface of the calm ocean.

"You're awake," a familiar voice sounded from the shadows.

"Captain Moby. Hello. I couldn't sleep."

"That's all right, nothing better than enjoying the serenity of the night sea."

Sunshine crawled up the stairs to the upper part of the deck where Captain Moby manned the helm of the ship. She looked out beyond the rails to see ocean stretching out in all directions. "Captain Moby," she said as she took a seat on the bench behind him. "Did you really catch sea monsters for my real dad?"

"Oh, yes. Some of the biggest, most vicious beasts that roam the sea. Ever since he was just a child, I would tell him the tales of my travels. Once he took charge of Darksmith Manor, he had me set sail to find the most dreadful and delightful demons of the deep. The Duke became an amazing man, created things your

Grandfather Damien never even imagined could have existed."

"Created things?" Sunshine asked. "What do you mean?"

Captain Moby turned from the wheel with a puzzled look on his face. "How much has Miss Adora told you of your family business?"

Sunshine thought about it for a bit and finally came to the realization that she really had no idea what she had gotten herself into. Captain Moby knelt down in front of her. "You, Sunshine, are the heiress to the greatest monster-making family there is. The five generations of the Darksmiths before you have been the main talent of creature creation and concoction that the world has ever known. Just about every bump in the night, all those things that should not be, every nightmare of nasty notions started off with a 'Made by Darksmith' stamp on its foot. And now, Sunshine, with your return, you'll be in charge of Darksmith Manor."

Chapter Three

The Towne of Munstro

Sunshine gripped Bunny's arm tightly as they ran past the trees of Wandering Willows. A maniacal laugh pierced the darkness, moving closer and closer with every step. Bunny flew from Sunshine's hand as she tripped and fell into the creek that ran behind the Saliente's house. She tried to pick herself up, but as she did, she sank deeper and deeper into the bottomless creek. She spotted Bunny floating in front of her and tried to swim to save her little, stuffed friend. She reached out, but before she could grab him, tentacles seized him from all sides and pulled Bunny into the darkness.

Sunshine felt a tug at the back of her shirt and gasped when something pulled her back into the air. The forest around her had changed. The trees around her had no leaves, no signs of life inside of them. The ground felt hot, as though fire had recently ravaged the forest. Sunshine turned to see what had lifted her from the water. Spit-covered fangs sat in a snarled mouth below the two yellow eyes of a wolf that stared down at her.

Sunshine fell back and then, louder than before, the laughter returned. She spun herself around to see flames form the outline of a gaping grin descending upon her. From above, a howl sliced through the air as the wolf leapt toward the flaming face and the two collided in midair. As they battled, Bunny walked up to Sunshine, took a deep breath, and bellowed out, "Land ho!"

Sunshine fell, panicked, from her cot aboard the Typhoonicane. The dream had left her shivering. She saw by the light that leaked in through the ceiling that her aunt was no longer in bed. Sunshine picked up Bunny, clutching him tightly, and found her way up to the deck.

"Morning, kiddo," Constance cheerfully greeted the little girl.

Sunshine ran up and hugged her aunt. "I had a real bad nightmare. There were monsters trying to get me and Bunny. I think they were gonna eat us."

Constance knelt down and put her hand on Sunshine's shoulder. "It's okay, Sunshine. It was just a dream."

Sunshine scrunched her eyebrows, looking up at Constance. "I don't want to make monsters. I don't want to make scary things that'll eat people."

Constance sat down on the deck next to Sunshine. "You don't need to make scary monsters. You can make them however you want. You're great-great-grandpa made monsters to help people. He made monsters that could lift up things that were too big for people, or monsters to help grow food. Once we get you settled, you'll be able to do whatever you want at Darksmith Manor."

"Captain Moby!" yelled the man from the upper deck. "The Towne of Munstro, something's wrong!"

Constance and Sunshine ran up to the bow of the ship to find Captain Moby looking through a telescope toward the far off shoreline. He turned quickly without acknowledging the girls' presence. "Pick up the pace, boys," he shouted. "Ol' Munstro's burning."

Captain Moby ran toward his quarters and signaled the girls to follow. "Sunshine, you stay in here until we can get a handle on all of this. Constance, you be ready for a scuffle as soon as we dock. For now, give me a hand with this."

Captain Moby reached for a large box on the top of a cabinet. Constance grabbed the other side to help him pull it down. Sunshine watched in awe as Captain Moby opened the lid and revealed a huge conch shell. The surface of the shell was coated in gold and decorated with diamond-like barnacles, the most brilliant the sea had to offer.

"What is it?" Sunshine asked in a whisper.

Captain Moby looked down at her. "We're calling the Leviathan."

Sunshine, left alone in the captain's quarters, tried to look out the small, round window to see whatever she could. "Do you see anything?" she asked her stuffed rabbit. Bunny stared back, unresponsive. "Me neither."

Just then, a tremendous wailing erupted from the deck of the ship. She looked at Bunny, looked at the door, looked at Bunny, and the decision was made. Sunshine and Bunny burst through the door to the deck. As quickly as they had gotten outside, Sunshine stopped in her tracks. Her face went pale.

Sunshine watched as a huge creature with the body of a shark and the face of some deranged bird crashed through the surface of the ocean. Ropes attached to harpoons that dotted its side danced like ribbons through the waves. The horn growing from its forehead was nearly the size of the Typhoonicane, and even the smallest tooth protruding from its monstrous mouth was bigger than the biggest member of Captain Moby's crew. It swam so fast alongside the ship that it nearly skimmed the surface of the sea. It quickly passed, heading toward shore and the Towne of Munstro.

"Couldn't stay put, could you," Captain Moby smiled down at Sunshine from the upper deck. "Can't blame you. Now, come up here quickly, so you can see."

Sunshine ran up to the bow of the ship and watched the Leviathan speed toward the seaside town. Captain Moby handed her the telescope, and she tried to find the town in the distance. When she finally focused on it, it was just in time to see the Leviathan turn sharply just before shore, and then, it came to a sudden stop.

"He stopped!" Sunshine called to the captain.

"*She* stopped," Captain Moby corrected. "Just wait and watch."

Sunshine did just that, and as she did, the ocean around the creature seemed to swell up. Then, all of the momentum from the charge toward the coast grew into an immense wave, surging toward the Towne of Munstro. The wave crashed against the sea wall, throwing water in every direction, dousing the flames that burned the stores and the spired cathedral that faced the sea.

"We'll be docking soon," Captain Moby yelled to everyone aboard the Typhoonicane. "Prepare to fight."

Sunshine watched once again through the small, round window of Captain Moby's quarters. Through the foggy glass, she could barely tell which was her aunt Constance among the others as they leapt down from the ship.

"Don't you worry about nothing, Miss Sunshine. Fid will keep you safe," said a massive sailor beside Sunshine.

Before heading off to help the townspeople, Captain Moby set Fid to stand guard over Sunshine. Fid, with a goatee as thick as his strange accent, was easily the biggest person Sunshine had seen in her entire life. One of the many tattoos on his arm was of a rabbit who looked somewhat similar to Sunshine's own Bunny, so Sunshine figured Fid, despite his menacing look, was a decent person. Sunshine walked up to Fid, seeking to find out the name of his tattooed rabbit. Before having a chance, a high-pitched squeal wailed just outside the cabin door.

Fid shouted, "Miss Sunshine! Hide!"

Sunshine scurried behind Captain Moby's desk and watched through a glass jar, half full of dried tentacles. Fid pinned himself against the door. Bang! Bang, bang! The pounding came to a halt as quickly as it had started. Sunshine peeked out at Fid. Before she could ask if whatever it was had gone, she spotted a glimmer of light reflecting off something near Fid's feet.

"Fid!" Sunshine screamed. "By your feet!"

Keeping one hand pressed to the door, Fid stood back to see what it was. Just as he did, a small chunk at the bottom of the door shot out. As it flew across the floor, Sunshine saw it was followed by something else. Something small and fast.

The little creature, some sort of reptilian rat, danced in victory in the center of the room, twirling his small knife above his head. Fid lunged at the creature, trying to grab it in his giant hand. It jumped away from Fid's grasp, landing on top of his back and jabbed the knife into his backside. It then leapt to the shelves where Captain Moby kept the case that held the shell used to call the Leviathan. The creature scurried along the shelf, knocking down whatever his little arms were strong enough to move. Fid got back to his feet and hurled himself toward the tiny terror. It easily dodged the monster of a man and then vaulted onto the desk, directly in front of Sunshine.

Without thinking, Sunshine grabbed the jar of dried tentacles and scooped up the little menace. She slammed on the lid of the jar and twisted it tight. The creature bounced around inside his glass prison, trying to escape. It then attacked the only thing it could, gobbling up Captain Moby's dried tentacles. Fid and Sunshine watched in stunned silence as the creature realized it had devoured more than it could handle. It grabbed its stomach and let out a monstrous belch. Appalled by its own stench, the

creature gasped for air and, then, passed out.

"Oh, no," Sunshine said, startled. "He needs air holes!"

"What?" Fid asked with a puzzled face.

"He needs air holes! So he can breathe! Use that knife."

Fid looked around, "What knife?"

He twisted to see where Sunshine was pointing and let out a yelp when he realized the knife was lodged squarely in his hindside.

Sunshine grabbed a piece of cloth from Captain Moby's desk and handed it to him. "Here. I'll pull it out, and you hold this on your bum."

He took the cloth, and Sunshine took the handle of the small blade. "Ready?" she asked.

Tears swelled up in Fid's eyes. "Ready …" Sunshine gave a tug, and Fid let out a shriek that rattled the jar holding the little creature.

Captain Moby, followed by Constance, entered his quarters. Fid, still guarding the door, kept the cloth firmly pressed against his wound. Sunshine sat at the desk, studying the little creature as he shambled about in a daze inside the glass jar.

Constance ran up to her, "Are you okay, Sunshine?"

"Yep. This guy got in, but we caught him."

Constance looked into the jar and scowled at the little creature. "Good, we might need this little gremlin traitor."

Sunshine had never seen her aunt so upset before. "What do you mean, 'traitor'?"

Constance walked around the desk and leaned down, giving Sunshine a kiss on the top of her head. "It's okay. There's someone we need to see."

Sunshine followed Constance as they walked down the pier toward the Towne of Munstro. Sunshine waved back to Captain Moby, "Bye! Thank you for the ride. It was very nice to meet all of you! Good luck at your restaurant!" Captain Moby, Fid, and the other members of the crew waved their good-byes back to the girls.

Sunshine skipped to catch up to Constance, holding Bunny under one arm and her little prisoner under the other. "Who are we going to see?"

Constance looked down to Sunshine, somewhat dismayed. "We're going to talk to the mayor."

As they walked through the town, Sunshine watched the people doing what they could to clean up after the attack. She tugged at Constance's arm. "Auntie Constance, can we help them?"

"We will, Sunshine. We're going to make sure nothing like this ever happens again."

"What did all this? Was it little guys, like this?" Sunshine asked, holding up the jar.

"Some of them. Other monsters, too." Constance knelt down to face Sunshine. "The monsters that did this ... they were tricked into it. Now that you're back, we're going to un-trick them, okay? We'll set things right."

Sunshine looked at the creature in the jar. "Did ... Mr. Fear trick them?" With that, the gremlin let out a laugh and began cheerfully bouncing around in his jar.

Constance and Sunshine continued along their way and approached the center of town to find a building that stood high above all the others. "I bet that's where we're going!" Sunshine smiled.

"Yeah. Yeah, it is. It's Munstro's town hall. That's where we'll find the mayor." A worried look swept across

Constance's face. "Listen, Sunshine. The mayor might not be too nice. The townspeople here have been pretty riled up since Fear began attacking villages, and they blame Darksmith. I think it might be best for everyone not to know who you really are for the time being. We just need to get some information from him." Constance licked her thumb and wiped some dirt off Sunshine's cheek before climbing the stairs to the town hall.

"Miss Constance Adora," the grisly-voiced mayor snarled from behind a long table. "I do not believe that now is an appropriate time for you, of all people, to be presenting yourself in the Towne of Munstro. As much as we do appreciate your help with this incident, I am sure you realize that the townspeople feel this could have been prevented long ago. Not only that, but it would probably have been simpler for us to just rebuild rather than to clean up the mess left by the sea captain's beast."

"Mayor Felix," Constance spoke clearly. "I'm sorry your town was attacked, but had there been an opportunity to prevent this, I can assure you that my people would have done just that. The reason I'm here is that I need help finding someone."

The mayor leaned forward and bore a dark stare into Constance's yellow eyes, "Finding some – " He finally noticed Sunshine hiding behind Constance.

"Who is that girl? Don't tell me your pack has turned to recruiting children?"

Constance scoffed at the mayor's accusation. "This is Sunshine Saliente, my niece."

Mayor Felix examined Sunshine briefly. "So, Flora had a child, did she? Good to see she's making use of her time in exile."

As Sunshine looked up at Constance, the mayor noticed the jar under her arm. "What is that you have there, dear?"

Constance stepped forward, "That's why we need your help. We caught one of the monsters that attacked earlier. If there's anyone in the world who is able to defend the Towne of Munstro against this threat, it would – "

The mayor raised his hand and stared at the little beast in the bottle, "I see where you're going with this, Miss Adora. Unfortunately, no one has had any contact with the doctor since Darksmith Manor was sealed. As far as we know, he was lost along with the Duke and Duchess. However, there is one – " The mayor stopped, glancing at the jar that Sunshine was carrying. "Little girl, please take yourself and that vile thing into the hallway. There are some things I'd prefer not to say in the presence of one of Fear's minions."

Sunshine sat between Bunny and the jar on a bench in the corridor. She picked up the jar and looked in at the little monster. "So, you're one of the bad guys, huh?" The creature sprang back and forth, scratching at the glass. "What's your name?" Panting, the little monster stopped and looked at the girl as though it had understood the question but didn't have an answer.

She picked up Bunny, and they both looked into the jar. The creature's eyes darted between the two of them. "Bunny, I don't think he has a name. We should give him a name, right?" The glass fogged up as the creature huffed and puffed inside. Sunshine tapped the glass, and a tiny hand wiped away some of the fog. Sunshine squinted, peering into the jar. "Hiccup! I'll name you Hiccup."

The creature reflected on his new name and soon began bouncing heartily in his jar. Sunshine tapped on the glass and Hiccup's bouncing came to a stop. "Now, listen, Hiccup. You did some real bad things. You stabbed my friend Fid in the butt, and your friends hurt people and broke stuff in the town. From now on, I want you to be good. You can't help Mr. Fear anymore, okay?"

Hiccup clapped his hands loud enough to make a tiny, quick noise that could be heard outside the jar. As Sunshine set the jar back down, a young boy entered the hallway.

"Is that one of the gremlins that attacked the town?" the well-dressed boy asked.

Sunshine set Bunny down and held up the jar for him to see, "Yep. I caught it on Captain Moby's ship."

The boy, who seemed to be a bit older than Sunshine yet small for his age, gazed into the jar in amazement. "What a wonderfully horrible little thing. Shall we kill it?"

Sunshine's jaw dropped, "What?! No, we can't do that. Why would you …"

The boy sighed and sat down beside her. Sunshine inched away, closer to Bunny. "Pity. My name is Yetzel Dragulus, by the way. My father is Mayor Felix Dragulus."

"I'm Sunshine Saliente," she told him hesitantly.

"Nice to meet you, Sunshine. So, what do you plan to do with this abomination?"

Sunshine frowned, "I don't know yet. I guess I'll just try to teach him to be good and to make up for the bad things he's done."

Yetzel sneered, "You couldn't possibly believe that, could you? Redemption for these fiends? Yes, I know that some may serve a useful purpose. Nevertheless, they most certainly should not be trusted more than they deserve.

They are evil at the core, and by the guidance of Fear, have completely given in to their wicked ways."

Just then, just as Sunshine decided she'd had enough of the mayor's son, Constance arrived in the hallway. "Come on, Sunshine. I think we'll be able to find the doctor."

Yetzel stood as Sunshine followed Constance out of the town hall. "It was nice to make your acquaintance, Sunshine Saliente. I am certain we'll meet again soon."

Trees, Trolls & Traps

A cool breeze cut through the heat of the afternoon sun as the girls followed the road south of the Towne of Munstro. Sunshine munched on an apple Constance had given her while she tried to see over the grassy field that grew beside the trail. "Where are we going?" she asked, disrupting the brushing sound of the blades of tall grass.

"We're going to find the lady who worked as head gardener of Darksmith Manor, Mum Furley. She and the doctor were good friends, so she may know where we can find him. Plus, if you're going to be running Darksmith now, it'll help to bring back some of the old gang."

Beyond the grassy fields, the road dwindled down to a dirt path where trees began to form a quiet forest. The sun, beginning to sink in the sky, barely shined through the thick branches to the leaf-covered ground. A while later, as if they had found the very middle of the forest, Sunshine saw the sky open back up. Basking in the day's last rays of sunlight were flowers and ferns and plants she had never seen before, all surrounding a small cottage painted in the pastel colors of her favorite kinds of candy. Some of the plants towered above the house, some carried the colors of a rainbow, and one … one with large, violet petals and vines stretching in all directions seemed to be running straight toward them.

"Auntie Constance!" Sunshine screamed.

Constance picked up Sunshine and shouted, "Hang on!" She ran back into the thickness of the forest, carrying Sunshine and racing parallel to the path. The plant broke through the forest edge, knocking down smaller trees as it chased the girls. Sunshine watched the jaws of the flower snapping just behind Constance's shoulder. She realized they were barely out of reach of the vicious vegetation as Constance leapt from tree to tree in the dense forest. Finally, with a short distance between the girls and their attacker, they hurled their way back onto the path, and turned, sprinting to the cottage.

The fiendish flower, now back in sight, whipped its vines at them, cracking the air. Constance skidded to a stop to avoid colliding with a stout, older woman wearing a soil-covered apron. Constance dropped to the ground, covering Sunshine's head with her hand. A blast of water shot over the girls' heads, crashing into the barbaric blossom and sending it tumbling root over petals.

"Inside, you two," Mum Furley ordered.

Sunshine looked in wonder as they set foot in the cottage. There appeared to be even more plants inside than there were outside. All different kinds and sizes, their colors spiraled around the room.

"He's really not so bad, you know," Mum Furley announced as she entered the cottage. "My guardian gardenia just hasn't seen too many new people lately." She checked a tea kettle, already heating up on the stove. "Now, Constance. To what do I owe the pleasure? I haven't seen you in ages. I trust you're still fighting the good fight?"

"Oh, yes. Always, Mum," Constance answered. "And that's why I'm here. This …" Constance placed her hand on Sunshine's head, " … is Sunshine Saliente, the daughter of Dominick and Delilah Darksmith."

Just so slightly, Mum's jaw dropped down. Then, moving in for a closer look, she smiled at Sunshine. "You've certainly grown into a sweet girl, haven't you dear." Mum walked back to the stove and prepared cups to be filled with her homemade tea. "So, I suppose we'll be moving

back to the manor?"

"It would help. The attacks by Fear are going to continue until he is stopped once and for all. If we can get him to set his sights back on Darksmith Manor, it would buy some time for the rest of the world. And once we've regrouped, we should be able to do something to end this mayhem."

Mum frowned, "We *should* be able to do something. But who knows if we could. Last time he came after Darksmith Manor, this poor girl lost both her parents. What if we can't stop him? What if he manages to finish what he started seven years ago? More and more of the Strays side with him every day. Who knows how big his horde of heathens has gotten? Even if we bring in all of your people to help defend the manor, we may not be able to stand up to him."

"That's why we need your help," Constance said, sniffing her cup of tea. "And Doc, too. If we can give Sunshine a crash course on what makes a Darksmith a Darksmith, wrangle up as many of the Strays as we can, and get some local help, we can handle Mr. Fear. We weren't prepared last time. This time, we will be."

Mum handed hot cups of tea to each of the girls and took a seat at the table. "Finding Doc should be possible. He was traveling in disguise for a while, entering science fairs and such, living off prize money. However, I know he has long missed his old laboratory and has been trying to find a way back into the manor. I believe he's been living in the hills south of Darksmith in order to keep an eye on the place and, maybe, come up with some ideas to sneak back in."

Constance glanced up from her tea with a questioning look, "He couldn't be in the southern hills. My people run regular patrols through there and have never turned up so much as a piece of scrap metal. Doc Bratenlager was never too quiet with his experiments."

"Well, of course not. Not in his own lab. No reason to be. Nevertheless, if he chooses to not be found by your pack, he is more than capable of doing so. Even if he's doing his best to hide, I think I have a few tricks up my sleeve to seek him out." Mum sipped the last of her tea, stood up from the table, and looked down at Sunshine. "Now, now. If you're going to be taking the reins at Darksmith Manor, I think now is a perfect time for you to start your training."

Sunshine cautiously followed Mum into the garden, keeping her eyes peeled for any plants that might leap from their pots. The oversized flower that had chased after her and Constance earlier was now sitting in a pot, snoring peacefully.

"Climb up here," Mum told Sunshine, pointing at a stepladder beside a tall, wooden table.

When Sunshine got up to where she could see, she found three small pots, each with sprouts growing. The sprout in the center pot looked normal - green, not too tall, not too short, nothing too special. The pot to the left held a yellow sprout that was growing ten times as high as the other two. The sprout in front of her was bright-red with a tiny, white flower at its top.

Mum shuffled through her supplies while Sunshine stood on the stepladder, eagerly awaiting her first lesson. "Alright, Sunshine," she said as she carefully squeezed an eyedropper to feed a yellow liquid into each pot. "These are outsprouts. They each do different things to help out in the garden. Go ahead and pull one of the sprouts out of the soil. Be careful and be sure to hold it tight."

Sunshine looked between the three pots, trying to decide which one to choose. She stretched her hand toward the red one with the white flower on top of it. She grabbed it just above the soil and gave a little tug. Before she could even get a good look at it, a tiny mouth, protruding from the root of the outsprout, began chomping at the air. Sunshine, amazed, stared at the onion-shaped root as it munched away at nothing.

"Careful, careful," Mum warned. "That outsprout is

used for crunching up rocks in the garden. Don't get your fingers too close or he might bite them right off."
"Now, Sunshine. I want you to tell him to stop biting."

Sunshine looked to Mum Furley, not understanding how she could get her savage little sprout to stop trying to gnaw off her fingers. "Hey, little guy," Sunshine whispered, searching for its eyes. "Please stop biting."

Immediately, the sprout gave up its attack. Sunshine set it down and watched in awe as the outsprout now seemed to wait patiently for her next command.

"You see," Mum chimed in, "Little beasties such as this will do whatever you want. You're a Darksmith. It's in your blood. You won't have as much control over many of the bigger ones. However, sometimes you may still have a bit of influence over them."

Sunshine looked at the outsprout. "Go back in your pot, please." The outsprout, using its flower as a grappling hook, pulled itself up to its pot and settled into the soil.

Sunshine looked at the other pots. "What do these do?"

"This one," Mum started as she pulled up a bucket of water, "takes care of any extra water in the garden." Gallon after gallon, Mum poured the water into the small pot holding the yellow sprout. It swelled up like a balloon and, once it was full, started spraying out a stream, watering all of the other plants around them.

"And this one?" Sunshine asked excitedly, looking at the plain, green sprout in the center pot.

A slight look of disgust wiped over Mum's face, "That one? We really shouldn't pluck that one up if we don't need to. The green outsprouts are used to keep vermin out of the garden."

Sunshine, too anxious to examine the strange plant, grabbed the outsprout, pulling it up from the pot. Mum cringed as Sunshine waited for something to happen. "Buuuurrrrp," a gaping mouth roared.

The stink of the belch caused Sunshine to gag and drop the plant onto the table. Nose wrinkled, she waved at the air around her. "Ooooh, that's how it works."

Mum picked up the outsprout and jammed it back into the pot. Stepping back from the noxious cloud, she looked to Sunshine, "Well, you had to know for yourself, I suppose." Mum checked her watch. "Now, now. That should be enough learning for tonight. We should get some sleep so that we may leave bright and early to seek out the good doctor."

The morning sun glimmered through the window onto

Sunshine's face, waking her up from her slumber in a large, cushioned chair. She heard Mum in the kitchen, humming as she prepared something that smelled even more amazing than the garden outside. Sunshine crawled down from the chair and sleepily tottered toward the kitchen.

"Good morning, Ms. Furley."

Mum, surprised to hear someone else awake, turned to Sunshine. "Good morning to you, Sunshine. But please, call me Mum. Food will be ready soon. If you'd be so kind to wake Constance, we'll be leaving right after breakfast."

After a meal of hot tea and syrup-soaked, berry-filled pancakes, the three of them headed out to the garden. The morning dew sparkled like stars on the foliage surrounding the small cottage. Mum walked up to a miniature, yet ancient, oak tree sitting in a massive pot in the center of the garden.

"Good morning, Buckley," Mum said, greeting the plant. "You'll be in charge while I'm gone, so get everything set to move out. I'll send word once we're ready."

Sunshine watched in disbelief as a withered old face in the bark of the tree turned up to face Mum. "Of course, m'lady. It will be a wonderful thing to return to the Darksmith grounds, give me a chance to stretch out my roots. Will you be taking any of the garden with you?"

"Just Venaticus to help carry some of our things." With that, a scruffy bush hopped out from in between some of the taller trees. The stout shrub ricocheted back and forth, running around Constance and Sunshine's legs.

Sunshine, seeing a chance to try out her newfound power over these strange creatures, shouted, "Sit!" Instantly, Venaticus stopped in his tracks, seeming to wait for a reward for good behavior. Sunshine looked to Constance, a bit caught off her guard.

"Auntie Constance, I think he wants a treat, but I don't have anything to give him." Constance reached into her bag, pulling out a canteen of water.

"Try this," she said, handing it down to Sunshine.

Sunshine opened the lid and splashed some onto the bush. Venaticus spun in a circle, each little leaf grabbing joyously at the drops of water as they flew through the air.

Heading toward the rising sun, they traveled along an unworn trail. Once in a while, the wind would stir the leaves of the tall trees, just loud enough to overcome the noise of Venaticus' branches rustling as he carried Bunny, the jar holding Hiccup, and some of Mum's personal belongings. They continued down the path all morning, every once in a while stopping for a snack.

A few hours into their hike, when the sun had crested in the sky, Constance dashed up to the front of the group. "Hang on," she said quickly. "The bridge is up ahead, isn't it?"

"Yes, not too far now," Mum answered.

Constance's eyes narrowed as she sniffed at the air. "There's something up there."

Venaticus stayed back with Hiccup, who was springing around frantically as the girls tiptoed closer to the bridge. Constance slowly unsheathed a silvery metal spike. Sunshine hid behind Mum as the sound of a brook babbling below the bridge reached her ears.

"Who's there?" Constance called out.

After a moment and still no answer, Sunshine, overwhelmed with curiosity, peaked out from behind Mum. Constance stepped within spitting distance of the bridge. "Show yourself," she shouted sternly. Sunshine's eyes widened as she saw the top of a stick poke up from below the bridge. They soon saw it was held up by a peculiar creature hobbling up the hill to the front of the wooden bridge.

"Grottum," Constance uttered under her breath.

Sunshine looked at the odd, little man to find he didn't

look much different than Hiccup, aside from being quite
a bit larger and quite a bit hairier. His face, wrinkled and
knobby and withered with age, stared at the girls through
a dirty pair of glasses with one missing lens.

"What are you doing here, Grottum?" Constance asked.
"I thought you kept to the bridge that leads to the
Haunts."

Grottum scratched his backside as he hobbled up to
Constance. "Well, it's good to see you, too, Connie," he
answered sarcastically. "No business going into the Haunts
'cept for folks that'd rather risk a curse than pay a toll.
And ol' Grottum's got to eat, right?"

Constance crossed her arms. "We're not paying you to get
across the bridge."

Grottum limped up to Constance, relying heavily on his
walking stick to make his way. "Now, Constance. You
know the rules. You don't pay the toll, trouble there will
be. Like I said, curses and whatnot. Totally out of my
control, you know." Grottum grinned a toothy grin as the
sun glistened off the slime that dribbled from his mouth.

Constance leaned down, face-to-face with the troll, and
smiled. "We're not gonna pay because we don't have to.
Sunshine, come here, please."

Sunshine looked up as Constance called her name,

breaking her stare from the crooked, old troll. Grottum stepped back, regarding the child, and then looked back to Constance. "What do you think, Connie? That you get some sort of discount because you have a kid with you?"

"Sunshine, please show Grottum your medallion."

Grottum watched Sunshine reach into her shirt, a puzzled look on his withered old face. Then, when the heirloom left to Sunshine by her mother, Delilah Darksmith, cleared her shirt collar, Grottum scratched his head in disbelief. He looked up to Constance for some acknowledgement that what he was seeing was real.

Constance gave him a slight nod, and Grottum burst into laughter, flinging his walking stick into the air. He took Sunshine by the hands and danced around in a circle with her, cackling hysterically. Finally out of breath, Grottum toppled over.

"Oh, oh," he panted. "This is wonderful. I always knew they would have gotten you somewhere safe." Grottum's head whipped toward Constance. "Are you girls going to open up the manor? And get rid of that pumpkin-faced goon once and for all?"

Constance nodded. "That's the plan."

Grottum clapped his hands and jumped back to his feet, his limp gone from memory. "Oh, good times, good times!" He smiled his brown-toothed smile at Sunshine and gave a mannerly bow. "Any lady of Darksmith and her guests are entitled to travel my passageways free of charge. Please, may your journey be safe and full of wonder. Ha! I haven't said that line in far too long. Now, please hurry along and do what you must, girls."

Venaticus joined the rest of the group as they lined up to cross the narrow, wooden bridge. "Now remember," Grottum said to Sunshine and Mum, "as soon as you hear the water rushing under the bridge to the Haunts, head north. Bratenlager is somewhere around there, I think. Connie'll probably catch the sound too early with her ears being as well-tuned as her folks are, so it'll be up to you two to hear it at the right time."

They all gave their thanks, said their good-byes to Grottum, and began heading across the bridge. Halfway to the other side, Sunshine stopped and turned around. "Mr. Grottum," she called out.

He looked up from making his way back below the bridge. Sunshine ran up to him as Mum and Constance tried to figure out what she was up to. "Mr. Grottum, you said before that you need to take tolls so you can eat. If we don't pay you, you won't be able to buy food."

Grottum stood up proudly, "For the Darksmith family, I

cannot ask for any payment. If I do not have funds for food, I will survive by that which the forest provides."

Sunshine looked dismayed, trying to think up a better compromise for the troll. Then, her eyes lit up, and she ran back down the bridge. After tussling around in Venaticus' branches, she returned to Grottum, holding her glass jar. "Mr. Grottum," she said happily, "this is Hiccup. He can help you find food. You can send him out for berries and things while you watch the bridge."

Sunshine unscrewed the lid of the jar, and Hiccup leapt out, scurrying to the handrail of the bridge. He let out a miniscule growl, bearing his sharp teeth.

"Hiccup," Sunshine said with stern expression, "You're going to be nice for Mr. Grottum." Hiccup groaned, and his upper lip twitched a bit. "You do whatever he tells you to, okay? You're gonna help him find food and things when he needs them."

Hiccup then shrugged and gave Sunshine a whimper and a measly salute.

"Ha," Grottum chuckled. "My very own gremlin. What a treat! Thank you, little Sunshine."

Sunshine rejoined Mum and Constance, and they

returned to their journey through the forest. Bored with the long walk, Sunshine had begun tossing Bunny up and down. "Are we there yet?" she asked, as she had been for the last few hours.

"Not much longer to go," Constance answered. "Once one of you hear the river, we'll be heading off the trail. You should be able to hear it soon. I caught the sound a while back."

Sunshine stopped playing with Bunny and ran up to Constance. "How come you can hear it? Is it because your ears are wolfy?"

"Sure thing," Constance said cheerfully. "I can even smell fish flopping around in the water from here."

"Wow," Sunshine looked at her in admiration. "Can you turn into a wolf whenever you want?"

"No, not yet. Just when there's a full moon. But even now, I have some of the gifts without changing."

Sunshine hugged Bunny. "How long have you been a werewolf, Auntie Constance?"

Constance took a moment to think about it, "I suppose since just a bit after you were born. I had always wanted to be one, though. It wasn't until Flora, your Momsy, moved away that I signed up for the change. It's been a rough ride, but I run with a good pack."

Sunshine tossed Bunny into the air, but as she reached up to catch him, the stuffed rabbit bounced off her hand and fell to the ground. "Oops!" As she crouched beside Bunny to pick him up, Sunshine squinted her eyes and cocked her head. "I hear the river!"

Branches snapped and dried leaves rustled as they trudged through the dense forest. To be sure that they could keep the river within earshot without his noisy interference, Mum had Venaticus trail farther back.

Constance turned to Mum, "How do you think we're going to find Doc in this?"

Mum pushed the thick brush out of her way. "I'm sure he'll find us first."

"Hopefully soon," Constance said in a tense voice. "The sun will be setting shortly." Soon after, darkness did begin to settle upon the forest.

Mum searched through a small pouch attached to her apron. By the dim glow of dusk, Sunshine shuffled up to her, trying to see what she was looking for. "Thought we may need these," Mum said as she squatted down, digging a wide hole into the dirt with one hand and holding whatever she had found with the other. She opened her hand to reveal three seeds, which she promptly plopped into the hole. "May I have your water, please, Constance?"

Constance handed her the canteen from her bag. Mum removed the top and sprinkled a few drops onto her freshly sown seeds. Though the water had barely a chance to soak into the ground, the seeds burst to life, instantly growing into three floppy, dinner plate hibiscus. Mum pulled up each of the glowing, pink flowers, roots and all. After shaking off the loose dirt, she handed one to each of the girls.

"Now," Mum said, beginning to demonstrate, "just take the flower, put it on your head, and tie the roots together at your chin. Sunshine and Constance followed Mum's lead. The soft light of flowers radiated throughout the forest.

Sunshine squinted, trying to see anything she could at the edge of the darkness, hoping to find a clue as to where they were going. She tugged at Constance's hand, "What are we looking for? Can't you just sniff him out?"

"I don't know," Constance answered. "Doc Bratenlager knows just about everything there is to know about monsters and creatures of the night and whatnot. So, I'm sure he knows just about everything to know on how to hide from them. Keep your eyes peeled for anything that looks out of place. If we don't find anything soon, we'll make camp for the night."

Sunshine pressed on in her hunt through the shadows until, finally ... "Shiny!"

Constance and Mum chased after Sunshine as she ran toward something buried in leaves that sent sparkles bouncing back from the light of their floral hats. When Sunshine got close to it, she paused, staring blankly at the mysterious, glittering thing.

"Careful," Constance warned as she and Mum caught up to Sunshine. As they saw what Sunshine had found, they fell into a trance, gazing at the crystal-like object.

"What is it?" Sunshine whispered, mesmerized as the pink glow of the flower on her head twinkled around her.

"I don't know," both Mum and Constance muttered with deadpan expressions.

Sunshine squatted down in front of it. "It ... looks like a star." She slowly reached out to touch it.

"Maybe you should be careful," Constance said, blankly.

Sunshine, still reaching for it, said, "Maybe I should." As she picked it up, Venaticus crashed through the bushes, causing the three of them to snap from their stupor. "Huh," Sunshine said, looking baffled at the very ordinary rock in her hand.

Constance, out of her daze, quickly put together what had just happened. "Trap!" she yelled.

The leaves surrounding them shot into the air as thick metal bars jetted from the ground. Constance tried to jump over the closing cage, but a steel roof spun down from the trees, knocking her to the ground and sealing all of them inside. Constance tried prying open the bars, but it was too late.

Venaticus scratched at the outside of the cage walls with his branches until settling behind Mum. She sat down on the ground, reaching through the metal bars and into her pack carried by Venaticus. She pulled out three oatmeal bars and handed one each to Sunshine and Constance. Making herself comfortable, she said, "I told you he'd find us first."

Chapter Five

Bumps in the Night

Sunshine pulled at the floppy petals of the hibiscus on her head, attempting to shield herself from the light rain that dripped down through the bars of the cage.

Constance stood along the side, looking through the metal bars. "Are you sure this is Doc's trap?"

Mum rose up from wet ground. "I'm sure it is. He used to do the same glimmering rock trick for holidays at the manor."

Constance shook some of the rain off like a wet dog, showering both Mum and Sunshine. "Sorry, reflex." Constance began pacing back and forth in the cage. "Well, it's good to see Doc has stayed sharp with his work. Hopefully, he shows up before the rain gets worse."

The rain did pick up as the light from their flowers started to dim. Sunshine, curled up by Venaticus and still pulling the faintly glowing petals around her head, watched Constance's nose twitch, searching for the scent of something in the darkness.

Just as Sunshine was about to drift to sleep, Constance jumped to the wall of the cage. Sunshine, jolted out of her drowsiness, scrambled to Constance's side. "Is something out there?"

They all watched in silence as two glowing, blue orbs floated through the darkness. The orbs' light drifted off them like mist on a pond as they moved closer and closer to the cage. Then, they stopped. The orbs sat there, hovering in the shadows, and suddenly, they disappeared. Just as the light vanished, the sound of crunching sticks and feet slapping the sopping-wet forest floor moved in on them.

"Woo-hoo!" The dark figure let out a howl as it reached the side of the cage. Then, by the last glimmer left in the flower on her head, Sunshine saw the dark figure emerge as an old man with white hair and a raincoat. He held a massive umbrella. It may have been just a regular-sized umbrella, but since he wasn't much taller than Sunshine, it looked huge by comparison.

"Doc Bratenlager!" Mum cheered.

"Mum, Constance, great to see you, but what are you doing in there?"

Constance, still holding the bars of the cage, "If you let us out, we'll tell you."

Doc Bratenlager chuckled, pulling his goggles down and flipping a switch on their side. They glowed blue. Now Sunshine could easily see they had formed the orb-like shapes that had appeared to float toward them. He searched through a bag. "It'll be in here somewhere. Ha!"

He pulled out a device with two big, red buttons and rows of lights along the side. Running several feet back from the cage, he yelled to the girls. "Okay, stand in the middle, duck and cover!" As they did, he pushed the buttons on the device. The roof of the cage spun back up through the branches overhead, vanishing from sight, and the bars that formed the walls retracted into the ground, hiding beneath the wet leaves.

Doc Bratenlager ran up to Mum and gave her a hug, "Ah, Mum, it's been too long. Been safe, staying out of trouble?"

Mum smiled at her old friend, "Oh, yes. Still have my garden to chase off anything that needs chasing off."

He turned to Constance, "And look at you, all grown up! Good to see the trap works, but I was expecting Ike or one of the boys." Doc's grin faded away when he looked to Constance's side to find a little girl staring up at him. He walked up to Sunshine and gave a slight gulp. "You look just like your mother when she was your age."

He looked up again at Constance, "We should get out of this rain."

The rain began to ease as they followed Doc Bratenlager through the forest. Soon, they arrived at a massive tree trunk. Doc dug through his bag again, this time pulling out a device with one green button in the middle and a small lever on the side.

"Okay, okay. Nobody move." Doc flicked the lever, then pushed the button. All of the sudden, a large, wooden basket plummeted down from the treetop, stopping just before crashing into the ground.

"All aboard!" Doc opened the door to the basket, and everyone climbed in.

Once again, Doc flicked the lever on his remote and pushed the button. This time, the basket began its steady ascent back up the enormous tree. As the basket rose above the surrounding trees, Doc pulled the goggles from his head and handed them to Sunshine. "You're not afraid of heights, are you?"

Sunshine shook her head as she took the goggles. Doc helped her put them on.

"I can't see anything," Sunshine said, pawing around at the air.

"Need to turn them on, first," Doc said as he flipped the switch on the side of the goggles. Everything lit up for Sunshine's eyes as if it was daytime.

She looked at Doc Bratenlager, who was illuminated by a gentle, blue light. "Pretty neat, huh? Now, come look at this."

Sunshine followed him to the edge of the basket. He held her arm as she climbed up into the seat. Looking out, she saw all across the horizon. Far off in the distance, she could see the buildings bordering the Towne of Munstro. The few lights that were on shimmered bright-white in the goggles. Then, to the north, she saw an enormous dome radiating a soft light and reflecting on the land surrounding it. Through the dome, she could make out a slight silhouette of what looked like a small palace.

Doc knelt beside her, "That, Sunshine Saliente, is Darksmith Manor."

At the top of the tree, the basket brought them to a round

door hidden in the bark. Doc pulled on one of the nearby branches, and the door opened, revealing a room full of machines. Gadgets blinked and hummed and buzzed in every nook and cranny. Wires weaved in and out of the wooden walls surrounding the makeshift laboratory.

"Quite the bachelor pad you've made for yourself," Mum said to Doc, smirking.

"Oh, this is nothing. Just enough to keep me occupied while the old lab is a no-go. But none of that matters anymore, does it? Sunshine, you have the Darksmith medallion, I'm guessing?"

She pulled the medallion out and showed it to Doc Bratenlager.

"Excellent," he said as he clapped his hands together. "We'll head over to the seal and pop that puppy open first thing tomorrow."

Doc sat on a wooden bench in front of Sunshine. "Must be pretty exciting for you, eh? Bringing back the glory of Darksmith Manor and putting an end to Fear, once and for all. Been a long time coming, I tell ya. So, any idea of what you'd like to make first?"

Sunshine sat down next to Doc. "What do you mean?"

Doc looked shocked, "Your first monster. It'll have to be

something tough, something that could help out if Fear shows up. You know, they say the first one you make sets the bar for things to come."

Sunshine sat back, thinking about what kind of wicked creature a little girl could summon up. "I don't know ... I had some spiders back home that were pretty nice to me."

"Ha!" Doc barked. "Good choice! Creepy, creepy. One time, your father and I put together a spider and one of the goats they keep down in Munstro. Not that bright of a critter. Kept eating his own web but, golly, did it look freaky."

Sunshine squeezed Bunny, trying not to picture what a spider-goat would look like.

Doc yawned, "Ah, well. We'll get to that tomorrow. There are some extra rooms downstairs that you girls can sleep in. Constance, in the morning, you may want to run off and round up your pack. Might take a couple days, though. Last I heard, they made camp on the east side of the mountains to keep watch over the Haunts."

"I'll wait outside," Constance responded. "If the clouds break up soon, I'll still have the full moon tonight. I may be able to cover most of the distance by dawn. Sunshine, will you be okay without me?" Sunshine nodded.

Constance headed outside after they all said their good

nights. Mum led Sunshine downstairs through the hollowed out tree to find a room to sleep. They soon discovered one with a mattress on the floor and various-sized boxes and scraps of metal strewn about. Mum smiled, "This is definitely Doc's place."

After a few hours of dreams filled with spider-goats and glowing eyes creeping toward her, Sunshine woke up in the dark storage room to find Mum still sleeping peacefully. Navigating past the boxes of odds and ends, she happened upon a small hole in the side of the tree.

Peeking out, she could see dawn trying to sneak into the sky as the early light bounced off the mirror-like dome cocooning Darksmith Manor. By the faint light that found its way into the room, Sunshine spotted the stairs back to Doc's temporary lab. She held Bunny by his stuffed paw as she snuck by the humming machines. After setting her rabbit on top of a tarnished, metallic table covered in wires and test tubes full of unearthly luminescent goo, Sunshine continue to explore, studying every contraption around.

Not having the slightest idea of what any of these devices could do, Sunshine's curiosity budded into temptation, her eyes widening at each brightly colored button and each little lever waiting to be pulled. Sunshine shook it off and dashed over to Bunny. "We shouldn't play …"

She noticed that Bunny's button eyes were fixed on the lever attached to the machine he sat upon. "But we don't know what it does," she whispered.

Sunshine's eyes darted back and forth between Bunny and the lever. She slyly snickered, "I have to learn sometime."

Her tiny fingers wrapped around the lever and gave it a tug. At once, blue and yellow and red lights flashed on and off. A loud alarm wailed. Sunshine fell back and watched in terror as straps fastened around her inanimate best friend. Bunny sat there motionless as three tubes, each fixed with needles, lowered down to him. The needles pierced his stuffed arms, and glowing liquid gushed through the tubes.

Doc and Mum burst into the room at the same time. Mum slid across the floor to Sunshine as Doc rushed to the machine. But it was too late.

Bunny's fabric skin expanded. Seams popped as he filled with the radiant ooze. As his furry body grew, bright-green smoke spewed out odors that knocked Doc to the floor.

Sunshine, being held by Mum, watched Bunny swell up until he was completely hidden by the cloud of bright-green smog. Then, the alarm stopped and for a split second that felt like eternity, there was complete silence. Suddenly, a roar thundered out from the cloud. Though they still couldn't see, they could hear huffing and puffing and panting and crashing as the machines around them were torn apart.

"Bunny," Sunshine whimpered. She panicked, terrified for her favorite toy and broke from Mum's grasp, "Bunny!"

Everything went silent. The cloud of green smoke dissipated and Sunshine found herself face to face with an enormous, blue-furred, button-eyed creature. "Bunny?" The big blue bunny gave Sunshine a tiny lick on the nose. "Bunny!" She jumped up and hugged the massive beast that was once no larger than a living rabbit.

Mum scrambled across the room to make sure Sunshine was safe and found her sitting gleefully on Bunny's shoulder, laughing with delight. Bunny grinned with a bucktoothed smile, carrying Sunshine in the same way she had carried him so many times before.

Doc ran to the machine that transformed Bunny into the hulking beast he had now become. "What?! That isn't supposed to do that! That machine was built to make meatloaf!"

Sunshine flinched as he spun around to face her. "How did you ...? How did he ...? What in the world did you ...?" Frustrated, Doc stomped his foot. "Never mind. Let's start the day."

Sunshine, riding piggyback on Bunny, followed Doc, Mum, and Venaticus through the forest. She could see light breaking at the edge of the trees in the distance and on the field that began just past it. Soon, they reached the end of the forest, not far from the seal that encapsulated Darksmith Manor.

Sunshine's eyes widened, and she shouted down to Bunny, "Giddy up!" Bunny hurtled toward the dome, using one hand to keep Sunshine from flying off his shoulders and the other to help launch himself faster and faster. Sunshine could hardly make out the shouts of Doc and Mum to slow down as they chased after them.

When they reached the dome, Sunshine could see the shadows of the manor beyond her own reflection. Doc and Mum arrived shortly after she had climbed down from Bunny and began examining the seal her father had created just before he had given his life to conceal her whereabouts from Fear. Sunshine tapped on it, hearing a sharp clink echo across the surface. She could feel warmth coursing through her hand as she touched it, despite the icy look of the giant dome.

"Can we break it?" Sunshine asked Doc, walking backward, away from the seal.

"No, no, no. But we can open it. However, once we do,

I have no doubt that word will soon reach Fear. When it does, he'll come for us, and we must be ready. We have a lot of work ahead of us."

Sunshine looked up at Bunny, her first monster creation and smiled. "We'll be ready."

Sunshine followed Doc's instructions and removed the medallion from around her neck. Slowly, she inched back toward the dome, holding out the only heirloom she had from her real parents. As she moved closer and closer, her hair began to stand on end. She could feel electricity traveling up her hand from the medallion. Then, quick streams of lightning crackled between the pendant and the seal. Sunshine jerked forward as the dome and medallion were drawn together like two magnets. Her grip came loose, and the medallion hovered on its own while digging itself into the side of the glassy dome.

Electricity shot far and wide across the seal, zigzagging over the entire structure. The bolts expanded and merged into one bright-white light, encasing it. In an instant, the light was gone. The medallion fell to the ground, and Sunshine looked up from it to see that the dome had vanished along with the light. Before her stood Darksmith Manor.

Doc picked up the medallion and placed it back around Sunshine's neck as she gazed in awe at the colossal, wooden-framed mansion. While trapped beneath the

dome, black vines had climbed up every wall of the building, breaking through windows and crumbling walls, reaching all the way to the roof. The eastern tower formed a crooked spire, twisting toward the sky. The other held a massive telescope, its glass eye peering at the Towne of Munstro. Each portion of Darksmith Manor seemed to have been built separately, each inspired by a different generation and hardly having anything to do with the previous ones. High above the main entrance, a skull, the same as that on Sunshine's medallion, stared down at her as they approached.

Doc patted her on the head, breaking her trance, "Welcome home."

Bunny's giant paw wrapped around Sunshine's hand as she led him through Darksmith Manor, exploring the home she had never known. They passed by portraits of unknown ancestors and statues of creatures that should only be found in the worst nightmares. Peeking in some of the rooms off the many halls, Sunshine found claw marks on walls, floors, and ceilings. Some rooms, containing rows of beds, were littered with shed fur, scales, and who knows what. What appeared to be a dining hall featured several long tables, each with silver platters every few feet, holding piles of broken, gnawed-upon bones.

Sunshine heard a soft clanging sound, which thankfully

broke the eerie silence. She followed the noise down a spiral staircase to find Doc banging away at a dust-covered contraption that towered over him. Light poured into the lab where the ceiling had once broken away.

"Come on, you little turd, start already," he yelled as he punched buttons and wrenched levers that hadn't moved in years.

"Hi, Doc. Can we help?"

"Don't know what good it'd do," Doc glowered. "Probably gonna have to replace most of these lines to get this place operational."

Sunshine shrugged as she looked up at Bunny. Bunny, studying the machine, reached out and gave the top a little pound. At last, lights throughout the laboratory flickered. Doc let out a hoot and zipped over to a handle on the wall. He jumped up to grab it, and as he came down, a swoosh of energy rushed to the flickering contraptions that filled the basement room.

"Good job, rabbit! Now we can get to work!"

Imitating Doc, Sunshine pulled her long, black rubber gloves tight, stretching them up to the elbows of her oversized, white lab coat.

After helping her adjust her goggles, Doc smiled at

Sunshine. "Look at you. Ready for the mad science of monster making! Don't mind the lab coat if it's a bit loose in the back and shoulders. Used to belong to my assistant, but we'll be getting one fit for you soon enough."

Sunshine gave him a thumbs-up and followed Doc to a long operating table. He pulled up a stepladder, and Sunshine climbed to the top of the table. She watched as he pulled a rolling metal cabinet closer to their workspace.

"All righty," Doc said, scratching his chin. "Let's see what we have to work with."

She tried to see what was in the cabinet but couldn't make out any of the things Doc had begun rifling through. She looked over her shoulder to check on Bunny, who had managed to get himself stuck in what looked like a giant hamster ball.

"Here we go!" Doc slammed a jar onto the table.

Sunshine leaned over and saw the jar was filled with black and brown bat wings. "What are we gonna do with those?"

Doc snickered as he pulled a gadget out from under the table and began pressing buttons. "We're going to make a monster. Simple one, of course. Actually a bit of a pointless critter, but a good place to learn the basics."

Doc grabbed hold of two hoses that hung from the ceiling. "Now, Sunshine. Pick out one of those wings and set it on the table.

"Okey dokey," she said as she pulled a leathery, brown wing from the jar.

"First things first. For the simplest monsters to make, you start with a base part. That would be this wing here, a severed hand, your stuffed rabbit, or something like that. To animate some mindless little minion like this, you need to give it a dose of the right ingredients and a nice jolt of lightning juice. These two hoses have your basic mix, concocted by yours truly and based on a recipe by your great granddaddy, Dante Darksmith. Now, go ahead and start it up." Doc handed Sunshine the hose with a small tree imprinted on the band above the handle.

She pointed it at the dried-up bat wing and gave the spout a twist. Chunky slime gushed from the hose.

"Okay," Doc shouted, almost instantly. "That's all you need."

Doc twisted the end of his hose, and a bolt of electricity zapped the ooze-covered wing.

Sunshine gasped as the little wing flittered like a fish out of water. Flapping with determination, it managed to take flight. For a moment, the bat wing danced sloppily in the air in front of Sunshine's face. She flinched as it suddenly shot into the air and ricocheted back and forth around the lab, until finding its way out the gaping hole in the ceiling. "Ha! Good work, Sunshine! Like I said, useless little critter but good practice."

Sunshine watched the tiny bat wing flutter away in the distant sky. Then, a stroke of genius flashed in her eyes. She hopped down from the table, ran to one of Doc's workbenches, and examined the various tools hanging from it. "Bunny!" she shouted. Bunny halted inside the giant plastic ball he had been running in, sending him flying upside-down when it popped open.

Once he finally stopped spinning, he dizzily lumbered over to Sunshine, who pointed and asked, "Can you reach that for me?"

Bunny grabbed a large pair of shears from the pegboard and handed them to Sunshine. Still trying to shake off the spins, he managed to find a place to sit on the stairs. Sunshine brought the shears to the table and tossed them on top.

"What are you doing?" Doc asked as she began shaking bat wings out of the jar and onto the shears.

"I've got an idea!"

"Well, you can't just throw anything together," Doc said

sternly as he tried to keep the hoses out of Sunshine's reach. "There's research, experiments that go into making these creatures. If we start to mix and match things just lying around, who knows what kind of freaky concoctions we'd end up with."

Sunshine, managing to snatch the hose with the tree imprint from Doc, gave him a wide smile. "This'll work." She blasted the bat wings and shears with the first hose.

As Doc tried to stop her, the ooze splashed to the ground just in time to catch his foot. He slipped and slid toward Sunshine, the second hose falling right into her hand.

"Oh? Thank you," she said, surprised. Firing a burst of electricity, Sunshine's eyes squinted with elated madness. She felt a warped joy watching her creation come to life. The joy bubbled out of her as a crazy, cackling laugh. Before giving the shears a chance to be carried off by their four flapping wings, she grabbed it from midair.

Pinning the creature to the table, her wide grin faded away as she regained her composure. "Hey, little Snippersnap. I have a job for you." She leaned in and whispered to the winged shears.

Doc returned to the table to see Sunshine's newest creation fly gracefully out of the lab on its task. "What?!" Doc exclaimed in disbelief. "That was way too much of the mix. It should have melted right through the table."

Sunshine crawled down from the stool and shrugged, "It was more stuff, so I figured I'd need more juice."

Doc sighed, wiping the ooze from his boot. "Well, you pulled it off, and that was one heck of a maniacal laugh you had going. Sounded like a genuine mad scientist!"

Sunshine giggled, "Yeah. I don't know what happened. I really got into it. But anyway, I sent him out to clean up the dirty old vines on the outside walls."

Doc nodded, "Good thinking. Get Darksmith Manor looking like it ought to."

Chapter Six

The Haunts

The next morning, Sunshine, Doc, and Bunny found Mum shuffling through her greenhouse, pushing aside pots and bags of dirt.

"What are you looking for?" Sunshine asked as she skipped up to her.

Mum lifted a box full of empty jars to show her. "It's been seven years since I last tended to my greenery. Most of the herbs and other ingredients have dried to dust. I've already sent Venaticus to retrieve Buckley and the other plants from the cottage, but I'd like to begin preparing further defenses for the manor."

Mum opened one of the jars. Bubbles floated up and as each of them popped, a fine dust wafted down and back into the jar. "I would need a whole new supply to build up our fortifications."

Sunshine pounced at the opportunity. "I can get more! Me and Bunny adventure all the time. We can find what you need!"

Mum looked to Doc as he shrugged to let her know it might not be a bad idea. Mum sighed, "Oh, Sunshine. You're sweet, but I don't know if you're ready to go wandering out to find some of the nasty things I need."

"Ho, hum," Doc shrugged. "I can go with her. Need to freshen up my stock as well. You make a list of what you need, I'll set my gadgets to autopilot, and we'll head off. So long as it's just the basics, you're shelves'll be filled by lunchtime."

Reluctantly, Mum agreed, and Sunshine bounced after Doc out the door of the greenhouse.

At the stairs to the lab, Doc turned to Sunshine. "Alright, munchkin. You head on down that hall to the West Tower, and you'll find whatever you want for our little trek. Won't need too much, I'm sure, probably just a basket or such, but something might catch your eye."

Sunshine pulled Bunny by the paw, past the dusty office where the business of Darksmith Manor had once been conducted. When they reached the West Tower, Sunshine and Bunny's eyes lit up. Strewn across the room

was everything anyone could ever want or need when stepping into uncertain perils. Net guns, grappling hooks, snorkels, and flashlights hung from the walls. Backpacks and traps of all sizes lined shelves. Sunshine immediately started digging into piles of random supplies, scooping up whatever might help on the forthcoming expedition.

Doc walked up the stairs from the lab to find Bunny and Sunshine waiting there for him. Sunshine was fully suited up in every shade of khaki and a pith helmet sitting on top of her head. Bunny, now a blue-furred warrior, carried a net big enough to catch even himself.

Doc tilted his head, squinting at the two of them, "Bit of overkill, eh? We're probably just gathering up some plants and little whatnots."

Sunshine looked to Bunny, then looked back to Doc and smiled, "Gotta be ready for anything!" Doc decided not to argue and led them back out to the greenhouse.

Mum came walking out the door as they arrived. "Here it is, here it is," she said, holding up a scrap of paper. "It should be all I need to get things started. You'll find most of it in the east woods, but the devil's foot only grows before the border to the Haunts."

Doc scowled, "The Haunts. Not too fond of heading that way. Never found anything there but trouble."

Sunshine tugged on the sleeve of Doc's lab coat, "What are the Haunts? People keep talking about them, but nobody has told me what they are."

Doc, taking the list from Mum, looked at Sunshine and Bunny, "A long, long time ago, there was a war in these parts. Most of the fighting went on in the Haunts. Ever since then, the whole area's been cursed, haunted, or whatever you'd care to call it. The worst of the worst kind of nasties lurking around there, they are."

Sunshine shrugged, "But if there are monsters, can't I just talk to them and tell them to be nice?"

Doc shook his head, "Not these, munchkin. They're naturals, born out of the wickedness in the world. Mutant hybrids, freaks of nature, that sort of thing. Many have been around since long before Darksmith. Last time I had to go through the Haunts, I got chased out by a whole herd of cows. Mind you, these weren't ordinary cows you'd find on a farm. These things were bigger than ol' Captain Moby's Typhoonicane, each one of them more bloodthirsty than the last. And they were just the young 'uns."

Sunshine kicked at the ground, "Shucks. I wanted to find more critters like Hiccup, the gremlin from Munstro."

Doc patted her on the back, "Soon enough, munchkin. First, we've got to get Darksmith Manor up to snuff."

Carrying Sunshine on a shoulder and a box of jars under his arm, Bunny marched behind Doc through the forest just east of Darksmith Manor. Sunshine peered through binoculars she had found in the West Tower, trying to spot items from Mum's list.

"I think I see the clothoberries!" Sunshine shouted to Doc.

Doc leaned back and shouted, "Those are just raspberries. You'll know the clothoberries when you see them."

Sunshine continued to scour the forest in search of clothoberries, devil's foot, and red semper trees, all of which she had never seen or heard of before. The forest was filled with mangy bushes and small, black, twisted trees trying to catch sunlight beneath towering trees whose branches kept the bright morning sun from reaching the ground.

She then spotted Doc, who was now standing in front of a wall of bark. Pulling the binoculars away from her face, Sunshine saw the wall of bark was just the base of one massive tree, looming over the forest. "Here we go, Sunshine," Doc yelled back.

Sunshine climbed down from Bunny's shoulder, using his giant net as a rope ladder. She ran to Doc to see which of the ingredients had been found.

Doc took a small knife from his bag. "Hand me one of those jars. This big son of a gun is a red semper tree. Mum uses the sap in the fertilizer for her crossbreeds. Adds some size to them."

Bunny handed over a jar as Doc jabbed his blade into the tree. Wind rushed through the treetops, causing an unearthly moan to fill the forest. Sunshine watched the sap ooze into the jar but kept one eye on the forest ceiling while she worked. The sticky goo continued to flow until they had filled three jars.

"That should be plenty," Doc said as he sealed the last jar. "Now, on to the devil's foot."

Sunshine, spooked, "But the devil's foot is by the Haunts. Shouldn't we find the clothoberries first?"

"No, no, no," Doc replied. "Clothoberries are finicky little things. Our best chance of finding them is to run into them by accident. So, might as well go pluck some devil's foot first and, if we're lucky, we'll just stumble upon the berries on our way." Sunshine relented and deeper into the forest they went.

As the trees became sparser and sparser, Sunshine could

feel her feet sinking into the damp ground. With each step they took, the light around them seemed to fade.

"Is it almost nighttime, already?" Sunshine asked.

"Nope," Doc answered. "That's just one of the things about this wretched place. Sucks the light right out of the day. Don't worry though, shouldn't get much darker than this."

Sunshine tried to adjust her eyes to the bluish-gray dimness that filled the air. Shortly after her sight had finally adjusted, Sunshine could make out a line of small trees in the distance. Tugging on Doc's arm, she pointed to the tree line.

"Good eye," he said softly. "That's the outer border to the Haunts. Should find plenty of devil's foot there. The story is, your great-great-grandpappy had devil's foot planted all along the boundary surrounding the Haunts. They say it's because the ghost of the old armies still duke it out, and he didn't want that mess spilling out any further than it already had."

The three made their way to the tree line. Beyond it, the forest appeared to have sunk completely into the marshy wetlands on the edge of the Haunts. Sunshine narrowed her eyes, trying to see if the shadows floating in the soft light were actually ghosts of fallen warriors.

"Psst," Doc whispered to Sunshine. "Stay close around here and grab a few of those jars."

Carefully, Doc removed one of the smaller plants from the ground.

"This is devil's foot?" Sunshine whispered.

"Yep," Doc answered. "You brought gloves, right?" Sunshine nodded. "Okay, I'll let you pluck the next one."

Sunshine brushed the soggy dirt away from the nearly exposed roots of the devil's foot. As she cautiously pulled it from the ground, the thin, long leaves twitched toward her face, threatening her with their tiny barbed spikes. Teeth clenched, Sunshine lowered the vicious plant into one of the jars, and Bunny twisted the lid tight.

"Good work, munchkin," Doc told her as he held the third plant.

Bunny swiftly answered with another jar, already open. "That should be enough of that," Doc said as he stood up, brushing himself off. "Oh, ho, ho, ho. Would you look at that."

Sunshine tried to see what had caught Doc's eye. He pulled out a pocket watch and then snapped his fingers. "We've got some time. Come along, now. I'll give you a sight to see."

Sunshine and Bunny chased after Doc, heading along the border of sickly trees and devil's foot. Soon, Bunny, who must have seen what they were running toward, scooped up both Sunshine and Doc in one arm. Sunshine, her face buried in the flailing flaps of Doc's lab coat, could only tell that they were now rushing up a hill. Finally, Bunny came to a stop and set the two down.

"Nicely done, rabbit. Now, Sunshine, take a look at that."

In the faint light, Sunshine could make out huge rock formations reaching into the sky, separated by miles of darkness. She could also see a small, dull glow bouncing through the fogginess, inching closer and closer to the edge of the border.

"What is that?" Sunshine asked Doc.

"They say those rocks used to be giants. They were so used to fighting that once the war ended, they didn't know what to do and just turned to stone. Supposedly, they'll turn back if the world gets bad enough, but I figure that's nothing more than nonsense folklore."

"Oh," Sunshine said, somewhat distracted. "But not the rocks. I meant that." She pointed at the light as it moved quickly toward the border of the Haunts.

"Not sure. Let's sit tight and see."

As the glow reached the border, they could make out the silhouette of a dark figure carrying a lantern. Stopping by the wall of devil's foot, the light turned sharply, racing in the direction of the ledge where Sunshine, Doc and Bunny were hiding. "Oh no," Sunshine whispered. "It's coming!"

Doc, crouching at the ridge, peered farther into the distance, "Another problem. He's not alone."

Sunshine's hand frantically dove into her bag as she remembered her binoculars. Pulling them to her face, she looked through the darkness, trying to see who was charging toward them. She gasped as she saw the pack of enormous creatures thrashing through the muck. Each one of their lizard-like bodies was held up by three legs on either side. Sunshine looked ahead of the pack of reptilian beasts and soon, she found the lantern carrier again. She watched as the dark outline holding the lantern ran through the swampy glop along the side of the devil's foot. Then, as the light hit his face, Sunshine dropped the binoculars.

"Doc!" she shouted as quietly as possible. "It's a little kid. He's being chased!"

Doc took the binoculars and checked for himself. He jumped to his feet, his eyes darting back and forth as he tried to devise some plan to rescue the boy. Simultaneously, he jotted down notes while shuffling through his pack.

Sunshine watched in fear while the lizard creatures began closing in on the boy. As they arrived just below the ledge of the cliff, Sunshine looked desperately to Bunny. Then, her eyes lit up, "Bunny!" she shouted, "Lean over the edge!"

As he hurried to follow her instructions, Sunshine rushed toward him. She pounced onto Bunny's back, pulling the giant net out of its sleeve.

"Catch me!" she shouted as she leapt over Bunny's head, diving past the edge of the cliff. As Bunny's furry paw gripped her ankle, Sunshine stretched out, reaching toward the ground and the boy as he ran below her. Using the net, she scooped him up, and the lantern flew to the ground, crashing against a fallen tree and sending flaming oil everywhere. Bunny pulled Sunshine up while she clenched the handle of the net as tightly as she could.

The lizard-things, unable to stop in time, slid into the fire, their greasy scales igniting instantly. Their slime-covered tongues flailed as they squirmed to try and extinguish the flames.

Sunshine, now safely back on the ledge, watched the giant beasts thrash about in the filth. Soon, they disappeared beneath the murky swamp water, leaving nothing but a trail of smoke behind them.

"Not the way I would have done it, but good job,

anyhow," Doc said as he approached the boy who was buried under the net's webbing. "Now, let's see who we have here."

Sunshine and Bunny watched as Doc pulled the net over the boy's head. Their jaws dropped at the same time. The boy helped Doc pull the net aside and looked at Sunshine. Sunshine stared as one black eye and one pale-gray eye blinked sheepishly at her and Bunny.

"Thank – " as the boy started, his lower jaw dislodged from his face. He quickly grabbed it and put it back in place.

Sunshine stared at his hand, which was missing patches of skin over the bare bones and rotting flesh.

"Thank you for that."

Sunshine stepped closer. "You're ... welcome," she said, slowly and quietly. "Are you ... okay?"

The boy straightened up his tattered clothes. "Thanks to you folks, I am. Don't know what I would have done had those skinkalisks caught up to me."

Sunshine stared at the scars and missing tissue on the boy's face, "No. I mean ... are you okay?" She motioned her hand in front of her face.

The boy cocked his head to the side with a puzzled look on his tattered face. "Oh!" the boy smiled. "That's alright. Always been that way, it has. Ever since the day I was born and crawled out of the dirt."

Sunshine, realizing the boy they had just rescued may not actually be living, looked to Doc to acknowledge that this was a normal thing. Doc shrugged and gave a slight nod.

"Oh," Sunshine looked at the boy, accepting his state of being, "Well, I'm Sunshine, this is Bunny, and that's Doc."

The boy smiled, bearing his decaying teeth. "Nice to meet you. I'm Cooper."

Back in the woods, Sunshine walked beside Cooper. "How come you were being chased by those things?"

Cooper looked at her in disbelief. "You haven't heard? The Haunts have been crazy, lately. Fear has been starting up all sorts of trouble with the surrounding villages. Even places as far out as St. Lucky's. Most of us don't want anything to do with it. We'd rather just keep to ourselves. But Fear, he's completely nutters. Lately, he just wants to ruin everything. Those of us who chose not to follow him have either been getting run off or added as the special ingredient to the night's supper."

"What are you gonna do now?" Sunshine asked.

Cooper shrugged, "Not sure yet. Thought about finding the werewolves since they'd probably be the first line of defense against Fear and his bunch. But from what I've heard, they don't take too kindly to Deadish types of folk."

Sunshine smiled, "My Auntie Constance is a werewolf! She would help you, even if you're ... Deadish. You can come with us and meet her when she gets back."

Cooper cringed, "I don't know if my walking into Munstro would be too good an idea. I heard stories from some of the ghouls back in the Haunts that had gone there once to try and set up some business. Got chased off by pitchforks and torches."

Sunshine frowned, "Oh. I'm sorry about your friends. But we're not going to Munstro. We're going to Darksmith Manor."

Cooper stopped in his tracks. "Darksmith Manor? We can't go there. The place has been sealed up forever, pretty much."

"Not anymore," Sunshine said, skipping ahead.

"But," Cooper uttered, catching up to Sunshine. "If Darksmith is open that means the heir is back."

"Yep, that's me," Sunshine told him, grinning.

Cooper's jaw dropped, once again separating from his face. "Thawtz …" he fixed his jaw, "That's you?"

"That's me," Sunshine answered.

"Are you nuts?" Cooper blurted out. "What are you doing so close to the Haunts? If Fear knew you were back, he'd send everything he had at Darksmith. There's no way anybody could stop him."

"I know," said Sunshine. "That's why we're out here. We had to get some ingredients to make some stuff to stop him from hurting anybody else. Then, we're gonna let him know we're here so he stops causing trouble with everybody."

Cooper looked dumbfounded at Sunshine, "But … you … you really think you can fight him? I mean, he's bad, really bad. If you're really the heir to Darksmith Manor, it's said that he's been trying to get you since the day you were born. Do you really know what you're up against?"

"It's okay," Sunshine told him, giving a half-hearted smile, "We'll be ready."

"Hurry along, kids!" Doc shouted, pushing branches of the thickening forest out of his way. "We still have the clothoberries to find before heading back."

Sunshine, back on her post atop Bunny's shoulder, surveyed the forest through her binoculars. Unable to find anything in the dense forest, Sunshine put the binoculars back in their pouch.

"I don't see – " she stopped as a sharp pain shot through her entire body. Then, she grabbed her nose and pinched it hard as she realized the source of the pain.

A stench filled the air, bringing even Bunny to his knees.

Cooper, baffled, watched the three of them gag. "What? What's going on?"

"You don't smell that?" Sunshine gasped.

"Oh. No, no. This thing's never worked," he said, pointing at his nose. "I mean, could you imagine? I'd have to go around all day smelling my own rot. Gross." Cooper looked alarmed, "Oh. Oh, no. You don't think it's me, do you?"

Sunshine shook her head. "No," her voice muffled beneath her hands, "You're not that bad."

Cooper smiled, "Well, that's good. But what do you …" He looked around, past the surrounding trees, trying to find the source of the vile stench. Facing the way they had just come from, his colorless face went even paler. "Hey, guys," he half whispered. "We should be running now!"

Bunny piled Sunshine, Cooper, and Doc all onto his shoulders. They gripped his fur as he whipped down the narrow path. Doc held the box of Mum's ingredients, trying to keep the bottles from flying out while Bunny hurtled over branches and trampled bushes that had grown onto the trail. Sunshine turned back to see that whatever it was had gained on them. Its red eyes looked out from beneath its gnarly, tangled, mud-colored knots of hair. About the same size as Bunny, the creature made its way through the trees with ease. Its long arms grabbed branches, launching it forward as it ran, occasionally falling to all fours and moving even faster.

Out of the corner of her eye, Sunshine saw the forest open to a small grove. Unfortunately, just as they reached a point where Bunny could speed up, the shaggy creature was already midair, its huge feet hovering just beyond Sunshine's reach.

As it crashed into Bunny, everyone went flying. Sunshine skidded across the ground and, for some reason, felt overjoyed. Light seemed to dance on everything around her. The gut-wrenching stench that had brought them to the ground seemed to have vanished, even as the creature stood face-to-face with Bunny.

Sunshine stood up, mesmerized by everything around her.

She watched in dazed awe as Bunny dove into the ape-like forest creature, tackling it to the ground.

Cooper pulled her to the side as the clash nearly rolled on top of her. "What are you doing?!" he screamed at her.

Sunshine marveled at Cooper's face as his wounds appeared to heal and color filled his cheeks. Doc, having salvaged all of the jars, scrambled over to the children.

"There's something wrong with her!" Cooper shouted.

Doc lifted her eye lids, taking a close look. Then, looking around the grove, he saw bushes growing throughout it. "Clothoberries! It's her first time around them, must be too much." Doc looked around, trying to find something to help her, then looked, intrigued, at Cooper.

Without warning, Doc poked a finger into Cooper's cheek, catching a smear of jelly-like goo on the end of his gloved finger. Cooper flinched, falling back. "Sorry, kid. But her head's flooded with life. Gotta even it out." Doc quickly wiped the slime on the end of her nose.

Sunshine jerked, jumping to her feet. Now, completely aware of what was happening, she stood paralyzed as Bunny battled with the abominable fiend. "We need to do something!" she yelled to the others.

Doc dove to his bag and pulled out a metal tube. The base

was filled with fork-like metal prongs. Falling to one knee, he took aim and fired the device. The forks, still attached to the tube by long wires, flew through the air, piercing the side of their target. The wires flashed as electricity surged through them into the beast. It let loose a howl and swiped at the forks, knocking them all to the ground. Sunshine leapt toward the box of jars, reaching in and pulling out one containing devil's foot. Just as she was about to throw the jar, her eyes widened in horror. Time seemed to slow down to a crawl, and she could feel the jar of devil's foot slowly rolling out of her hand.

"Bunny!" she screamed as cotton fluff exploded from his shoulder. The creature carelessly tossed Bunny's arm across the grove. Sunshine watched helplessly as it bounced along the ground. Suddenly, just beyond where the arm lay, a dark streak sped toward the monster. Sunshine realized it was a wolf as it and the hairy monster collided in blur of flying fur. Like her now disfigured Bunny, she saw that the wolf was also missing a limb.

With the hairy beast now focused on the three-legged wolf, Sunshine ran to Bunny. She pulled at him, trying to get him away from the brawl and was soon relieved to see a familiar face racing toward them.

"Auntie Constance!" Sunshine shouted.

Constance picked up the severed arm and ran toward Sunshine and Bunny. "Come, quick! Ike can take care of the sasquatch. His brothers will be here soon enough, so he'll be fine."

Doc, carrying the box of jars and several branches of the clothoberry bushes, raced over to Constance, Sunshine, and Bunny. "I've got the berries, so if you all don't mind, let's get the heck out of here."

Cooper ran up to them, also with an armful of berry branches, "I've got some …" Constance turned toward Cooper and, without warning, rushed toward him.

Cooper froze, " … I'm with them." Constance looked to Sunshine, who returned with a quick, nervous nod. Constance let out a slight growl and turned back to lead the others out of the clothoberry grove.

Slowing their pace, Sunshine caught up with Constance, who was talking to Doc. " … probably tomorrow. And even if he doesn't finish it off, he'll probably still head east. Right past Darksmith."

"What's tomorrow?" Sunshine chimed in.

Constance looked to Doc, as if for permission. "My friend, Ike, the wolf back there, had gotten word that Fear was still near the Towne of Munstro, waiting to finish what he had started before we arrived with Captain Moby.

It won't be long after that, that he'll find out Darksmith is back in business. If he doesn't find out sooner." Constance glared back at Cooper.

Sunshine, scratching her head, asked, "Can't we just make a bunch of monsters when we get back and go help the Munstro people? We've got everything from Mum's list."

"We do," said Doc, "Unfortunately, these are mostly used to set up defenses for the manor. Had to make that the top priority for the time being."

"Couldn't we find more monsters to help?" Sunshine asked. "Like the Strays?"

Constance frowned, "Probably not enough time. At least, not enough time to find folks we can definitely trust. We've already joined forces with the walking dead, and that's bad enough."

Sunshine looked dismayed, "How come you don't like him?"

Doc butted in, "Some things can best be explained at a later time. And Constance, try to be nice. The boy should be just fine."

The sun sat high in the sky as Darksmith Manor came

within sight. Sunshine skipped ahead and looked over the acres and acres of fields that rested peacefully in front of her new home.

"I think we can do this," she said, turning to Doc and Constance. "I think we can help the Towne of Munstro and stop Mr. Fear. Even if there's not a lot of time, we can get some stuff done. We've got enough of our friends, and we can all help out. As long as we can get Darksmith Manor safe and sound, we just need to let him know we're here and make him bring the fight to us."

Doc laughed and patted her on the head. "What do ya know? You're already talking like a true Darksmith."

Chapter Seven

Cobwebs & Craniums

"You two, come with me," Doc shouted to Cooper and Bunny as they hurried into the front entrance of Darksmith Manor. "We'll see about getting that arm back on. Constance, can you take the box of jars back to Mum? Let her know it's gonna be a late night." Doc, Cooper, and Bunny disappeared beyond the door.

"No prob – " Constance paused, transfixed by something in front of her. Sunshine saw a black cloud whirling out from thin air in front of them. The two of them froze, Constance sliding her weapon from its sheath.

"No need for that, child," a voice eerily uttered from clearing smoke.

"Mr. Death!" Sunshine cheered. From the darkness emerged the hooded skull of Death.

"I apologize for my tardiness, but I am bound to my responsibilities. Now, I understand you are preparing to face Fear and his minions."

"We have to," Sunshine began to explain. "He's gonna go after the Towne of Munstro, so we're going to help them out and kick his butt. Will you help us?"

Death bowed down to Sunshine, "Of course, my young Lady Darksmith. And even now, your forces grow strong." His skeletal hand rose up, aiming toward the southern forest. Sunshine and Constance looked in the direction that his bony finger pointed.

"What is that?" Sunshine's voice quivered.

A section of the forest seemed to move toward Darksmith Manor. Branches of trees and vines reached out, closer and closer.

"Mum's plants," Sunshine realized, "from the cottage. It's Venaticus and Buckley and the others!"

Sunshine handed the box of jars to Constance. "I'll let her know they're here," Constance said, taking the box and heading around the manor to the greenhouse.

Venaticus reached them first, hopping and running circles around Sunshine's legs. While trying to calm him down, she looked up to Death.

"Mr. Death, you can poof, disappear and go anywhere, right?" Death gave her a nod. "Could you find the Strays? The ones that would want to come back to Darksmith Manor and could help us. If we let them know it's opened back up, they might want to come back, right?"

"I believe they would, Sunshine, and I will do just that. However, I sense the sands of time may be running low on the lives of many of the residents of the Towne of Munstro. Even if I could reach all of the former inhabitants of Darksmith Manor, it is doubtful they would arrive in time. I will seek out those within reach and return back here to further assist in your preparations." Sunshine thanked Death as black plumes of smoke spiraled around him. Then, Death was gone once again.

Cooper shrieked in pain as Bunny clenched his hand. Sunshine cringed as she tried to keep his massive, severed arm held upright.

"Just one … more … stitch," Doc said, threading a shoelace-sized string through the giant rabbit's fur to reattach the torn off arm. "There! All set."

Bunny sat up from the operating table, wiggling the fingers of his recently detached arm. Green tears flowed down Cooper's cheeks as he clutched his hand. "Couldn't we have just strapped him down?"

"Buck up, my festering little friend," Doc told him, cheerfully. "You'll be fine in no time."

"Okay," Doc said, clapping his hands. "Ol' Mum is taking care of the fortifications. Constance has probably moved on to prepping the artillery. As for you kids, you're going to the dungeon."

"What?!" Cooper blurted out, still clenching his sore hand.

Sunshine's eyes lit up, "We have a dungeon?"

"Yes, yes, we do," Doc answered as he walked over to a large brick wall, the only one in the lab that wasn't adorned with some sort of buzzing gizmo. Pulling down on the candlestick that hung from the wall, the bricks slid back and opened to reveal a dusty, but exceptionally large elevator. "Not too bad of a dungeon, either. You're grandpappy had mostly used it for storage. Anyhoo, you three head on down there and see what you can dig up. I know you haven't been at this too long, Sunshine, but I expect instinct will kick in and point you in the right direction."

Sunshine, Cooper, and Bunny filed into the elevator. Doc, handing each of them lanterns, gave them a slightly uneasy look. "Not that you should run into any trouble down there, but we used to, every once in awhile, have some unwelcome guests in the dungeons. Should've

all cleared out when the seal locked the place up, but
something may have weaseled its way in. Doubt it. Just
thought you should know." Cooper looked nervously at
Sunshine as Doc pulled on the candlestick. "Have fun!"

Sunshine and Cooper crept ahead of Bunny through
the dark, dank dungeon. The light from their lanterns
flickered as they passed by empty cells, each one seeming
larger than the last.

"What do you suppose we'll find?" Cooper asked.

"Not sure," Sunshine whispered back. "I guess we'll just
know it when we find it."

As they made their way beyond the first corridor, they
entered a huge, dome-shaped room. "Wow," Sunshine
looked around in awe, her lantern's glow not even
reaching out to the farthest walls. Strewn throughout
the room were massive, wooden contraptions and chains
hanging down from the ceiling. Gears, spikes and shackles
adorned the medieval-looking cages and racks. Sunshine
walked over to a large, round machine in the center of the
room.

Cautiously, she took hold of the crank on the side of the
device. Rotating it just once, the machine launched into
a blinding spin. Sunshine stumbled back, colliding into

Cooper and knocking both of them onto the ground.

"I've heard stories about this room," he said as he picked himself up. "They call it the Purgatorium. The Darksmiths used it for making the not-so-bad monsters a little bit worse. Maybe we shouldn't touch any of these things."

"Umm, yeah. Maybe not." Sunshine stepped farther back as the spinning torture rack began to slow down. "I know these things are bad, but if we slowed that one down, it could probably be pretty fun."

Cooper looked at Sunshine, a bit concerned but then looked back at the whirling machine and shrugged. "Maybe it could."

As they moved deeper into the dungeon, wooden crates began to fill the empty space. Sunshine spotted a crowbar beside one of them, grabbed it, and handed it to Bunny. "Let's open some of these up. Maybe we'll find something useful inside."

Bunny pried open the crate, and dust spewed out all over his feet.

"Bones," Sunshine said as she peeked into the crate.

Cooper examined the contents of the crate. "It looks like it's just a bunch of leg bones and toes. Maybe we can make some sort of centipede critter."

Sunshine thought to herself for a moment. "We would need a big wormy thingamajig or a snake or something for that, I'd think. Let's check the boxes for other bones, and maybe we can put together skeletons."

Cooper and Sunshine dug through more crates as Bunny popped them open. Each contained more and more bones they could piece together.

"Well," Sunshine said, looking over the open crates. "That's everything except for their heads. Let's use that twirligig to set them up, and then we'll try to find the skulls."

Bunny stacked the crates and pushed them down the hall into the dome-shaped room. Cooper, walking backward as he led the way, looked to Sunshine. "Maybe the skulls are down one of the other hallways. We should find more crowbars and – " His words were cut off as he flew straight up into the air.

Sunshine ran forward, trying to see what had happened. "Cooper!" she yelled. Above her, he whipped around the ceiling of the dome, being pulled by some unseen force. Bunny appeared at Sunshine's side, watching their Deadish companion flying through the air. Finally swinging to a stop, Cooper looked around as he hovered above the others.

"It's a …" his voice shuddered, "it's a spiderweb. I'm in a spiderweb!"

"We'll get you out, don't worry," Sunshine called up to him.

"Guys," Cooper hissed, almost too quiet too hear.

One by one, eight gargantuan legs shuffled across the ceiling until they reached the sticky web. The dim light of the lanterns bounced off the spider's hairy back. Cooper screamed as the web shook, and its maker loomed forward.

Sunshine grabbed Bunny by the arm. "Throw me," she said, desperation in her voice. "Throw me up there, into the web."

Bunny's brow furrowed, but then, he picked Sunshine up in one of his massive paws. She curled into a ball and yelled, "Do it!" Bunny did and let her fly.

Sunshine whizzed toward the ceiling. Springing against the sticky, elastic cords, she was pinned to the web, feet over head. Upside down, Sunshine looked around, trying to find Cooper and the gigantic spider.

"What are you doing?" Cooper shouted. "Now we're both stuck." Sunshine twisted, following the sound of his voice. Nearby were the multiple eyes of the beast creeping

toward Cooper.

Reaching into her shirt, Sunshine clutched the Darksmith medallion. She pulled it out and held it toward the spider. "You cut it out! Let us down from here."

Its eight eyes blinked simultaneously. Sunshine, still holding out the pendant, stared at the spider. "Please," she murmured.

The atrocious arachnid charged at her. Sunshine closed her eyes as she tried to tuck her head into her chest. She could feel herself spinning as webs wrapped around her. Then, unexpectedly, she heard a laugh and felt herself floating. Peeking out with one eye, she saw Cooper hanging next to her, his upside down face grinning as he looked around.

Sunshine was amazed as the vicious-looking creature gently lowered them to the floor of the Purgatorium. Reaching it, Sunshine hopped back to her feet and untangled her sticky shroud.

"Thanks," she said to the spider. After pulling off the last of the webbing, she spun around to Bunny. "I have an idea. You two go find the skulls. Me and our new friend can set up what we already have."

Cooper, still peeling off the webs, stared at Sunshine, "Uh, are you sure?"

Sunshine looked back at the giant spider. "Yeah. I think it'll be okay."

Not much later, Sunshine looked up to see two lanterns enter the dome-shaped room.

"We found them," Cooper called out while Bunny lugged the final box to Sunshine.

"Great," Sunshine replied. "Check out what me and Crazy Legs here did."

Eleven headless skeletons hung in cobweb shackles from the machine in the center of the room. Their bones bound together by the sticky webbing of the spider that loomed over the small girl.

"This twirligig should be able to fit in the elevator. So, as long as we can push it over there, we can bring it right up to Doc to help us with our boney buddies."

Cooper placed one of the skulls on an incomplete skeleton and scooped up a heap of webbing to hold it in place. "Wait," Cooper said, pausing in his work. "Did you say Crazy Legs?"

Sunshine smirked, "Yeah. The spider. Look at his legs. They're crazy."

"Oh. Okay."

With all of the skulls in place, Sunshine and Cooper led the way through the dungeon. Crazy Legs dragged the front of the twirligig, tugging the towline of his own webbing while Bunny pushed from the back. The worn, old machine creaked and squeaked as it squeezed between the empty cells. Finally reaching the elevator, Crazy Legs climbed over the contraption to help Bunny give the final shove. Sunshine, sitting with Cooper between two of the strung up skeletons, patted one the spider's eight hairy legs.

"Thank you for your help, Crazy Legs. You're not gonna be able to fit for the ride back up, but I'll be sure to come and visit you as soon as I can." With that, the spider jumped up, flipped onto the ceiling and scurried away, into the shadows. Bunny squeezed onto the elevator, hit the switch, and up they went.

Back in Doc Bratenlager's laboratory, Bunny jerked the twirligig off the elevator.

"Doc," Sunshine called into the empty room. "Doc, where are …?" A metal chamber in the far corner of the lab buzzed abruptly. Steam shot out from the windowless door as it slid open and an indistinct figure emerged from the haze. "Doc?" Sunshine asked, not sure if that was who stood before her.

"Right, you are, munchkin." Doc stepped out from the cloud, holding a glass canister.

"What is that?" Sunshine asked, staring into the swirling purple and black cloud that danced inside the clear container.

"This," Doc held it up for her to get a closer look, "is life. Spirits made from the world itself. Refined from the finest ingredients ever collected by Darksmith Manor. Combine this with the right stuff, and you, m'lady, can forge the kind of blue-ribbon beasts that your predecessors would be proud of. If we're going to end this scuffle with Fear, this is how we'll do it."

"Can we use it on these?" Sunshine asked, pointing to the eleven skeletons. Doc, examining the twirligig's occupants, gave Sunshine a deranged grin, "We sure can."

Sunshine and Cooper stood in front of Bunny, watching Doc dig through the twirligig's control panel at the base of the machine. He rapidly attached multi-colored wires and cords.

Sunshine tiptoed over to Doc, "Do you need any help?" Doc looked upside down at her from between his legs. "Yeah. Why don't you go ahead and bring me that canister."

She ran over and scooped up the can of spirits. "Okay, okay," Doc said, taking the canister. He twisted it into place in a small hole next to the main crank on the twirligig. "Now that that's that, give 'er a whirl."

Sunshine took the crank in hand and, this time more cautious than the first, nervously turned it clockwise. Despite her best efforts, the machine fired into a rapid spin, the skeletons' webbed shackles barely kept them attached. In the canister, tiny streams of lightning danced throughout the mysterious fluid. Sunshine, Cooper, and Bunny all tried to keep their eyes up to speed, watching the skeletons zip by.

Doc pushed a small button on the canister, and the liquid's glow faded away. "We won't need too much," he yelled over the gyrating machine. "Skellies are simple enough to pull off. Your grandpappy and I once had a whole factory for this out east. We could do hundreds and hundreds everyday, s'long as we had the bones. Got to the point where some places had more skellies than regular folk walking around." Finally, the machine slowed to a stop, the skeletons hanging there as lifeless as they were when they started.

"Didn't it work?" Sunshine asked, let down by the motionless bones.

Doc scratched his temple, "Hmrph. These bags of bones should be bouncing all over the place by now." Doc poked and prodded the cables in the control panel's inner workings. "That goes there, this goes here. Hmm. Should be working just fine."

Sunshine sat on a stool beside the operating table with a look of disappointment on her face. "Maybe I'm not ready for big stuff yet." Bunny tapped her on the shoulder, pointing at himself and nodding happily.

Sunshine petted his paw. "I guess I just got lucky with you. I suppose we could make more little bat-wing thingies."

"No can do," Doc said. "Used up the bat wings on that Snippersnap you made. There's gotta be something screwy here. How about you kids go have yourselves something to eat while I try to work it out." Eager to fill their rumbling stomachs, they hopped to their feet and headed up to the kitchen.

On the way to the kitchen, they found the dining room table overflowing with a feast of fruits and vegetables. Immediately, Bunny swiped up a paw of absurdly large carrots and began gobbling them up.

"Mum must've done this," Sunshine said, picking up an apple as big as her head. She took a seat next to Bunny as Cooper continued to look through the pile of food.

"Eh," he grumbled. "It all looks a bit fresh for my tastes. I'll go check the pantry for any leftovers from before this place was sealed up." Cooper scampered off while Sunshine and Bunny chomped away at their lunch.

Not even a quarter of the way done with her apple, Sunshine set it on the table and slowly slid deeper into her chair. "That was ... awesome. Do you want the rest?" she asked, looking up at Bunny. With a quick scoop of his paw, he grabbed the apple, wolfed it down, and moved on to a head of lettuce on his plate.

"Bunny," Sunshine whimpered, almost in a sigh. "I feel bad about the skellies. I know it must have been my fault they didn't work. Something just didn't feel the same, you know? Like when I made the Snippersnap. Or with you, even though that was an accident. This time was different, like something was missing."

"Something *was* missing." Sunshine turned toward the ominous voice to see the tall, hooded figure.

"Mr. Death!" Sunshine said, surprised, looking up to his bony face as he walked around the table, taking a seat across from her.

"When the founder of this place, Damarcus Darksmith, first began manufacturing creatures of the night, I became aware of an unprecedented situation. These beasts, once deceased, had no place to go. The rules of the afterlife, already set in stone, have no flexibility to allow these abominations of the natural order to carry over. Hence, I was charged with the task of establishing such a place, lest these creatures wander the hereafter in limbo."

Sunshine, crouched on the edge of her seat. "So, what did you do?"

"That is when I first met Damarcus. This, being prior to the War of Fang and Fur, and prior to Damarcus' lust for wealth. In order to complete my task, I had to understand the process by which these fiends were made. I soon learned that the ingredients that constituted the monsters of Darksmith played only a minor role. More importantly is what your forefathers have come to call the Madness."

Sunshine perked up, listening more intently than ever. "The Madness, as described to me by all the generations of the Darksmiths, is something … something buried deep in the mind. Almost a foresight to envision their design and the ability to bring it forth. By tapping into this Madness, the Darksmiths have been able to harness its power, and, by combining it with their ingenuity, slip the essence of life into these beasts."

"Through the guidance of Damarcus, I was able to channel the power of the Madness, using it to create Nocnitia, the resting ground for the souls of monsters." Sunshine raised her hand. "Yes, child?" Death asked.

"Where is Nocnitia?"

Death looked up, pondering the answer. "If a location could be given, it would be somewhere between life and dreams. During the worst nightmares one may have, a person may witness a glimpse of what lies in Nocnitia. What is important now, is that you learn to find the Madness within yourself. Once you have, you will possess the unique ability to create the beasts of Darksmith Manor."

The door from the kitchen swung open. "I found meat!" Cooper cheered, holding a handful of jerky, covered in patches of gray fuzz. "Oh," he paused, seeing the cloaked skull looking at him. "You must be one of the skellies. How'd you get that to work, Sunshine?"

Sunshine hopped down from her chair. "He's not one of the skellies. This is Mr. Death."

Cooper froze, mouthful of moldy jerky. "Mr. Death?" he mumbled. Then, looking startled, "The Grim Reaper, Death?"

"Yep," Sunshine answered.

"Oh," Cooper nervously began backing away. "You're not here to …"

Death laughed. "You Deadish are always so nervous upon

meeting me. Worry not, I haven't come to reclaim you. As far as I am concerned, once born Deadish, you are entitled to your second chance at life."

"Oh," Cooper murmured after gulping down his chunk of jerky. "Um, thanks."

As Cooper sat down beside Death, Constance entered the room. Following behind her was a man, his long, light-brown hair being held back by a green headband with a pale-blue crescent moon in the center of it. His yellow eyes sat droopingly behind the round, red lenses of his glasses. The right sleeve of his jacket was rolled up and pinned, missing the arm that ought to have been there.

"Everyone," Constance said quickly. "This is Ike. He and his brothers are from my pack. The others are in the West Tower making preparations."

"Nice to meet you," Sunshine said as she walked up to shake his hand.

"You must be Sunshine," Ike said, his voice sounded as relaxed as a voice could be. "So, you're the big cheese now. Far out, little lady."

Constance headed toward the hallway. "I'm going to gather up Doc and Mum, we'll be leaving for Munstro sooner than later."

Sunshine climbed onto a chair to sit beside Ike. "So you're a werewolf, too?" she asked him.

"Heck yeah, Sunshine. Matter of fact, day you were born, you and Constance saddled up on my back for a ride."

"Really?" Sunshine asked.

"Sure thing," Ike said, his right shoulder moved under the rolled up sleeve, as if to gesture with his missing hand. "That was one crazy day. Even lost my arm on that trip."

"Oh, no. I'm sorry."

"Nah," Ike said waving at the air with his remaining hand. "Ever since then, I've been able to wolf out whenever. Don't even need a full moon. It usually takes a decade or more to get to that point. That's how we get these." Ike pointed to the crescent moon shape that was embroidered onto his headband. "Out of all the packs out there, there are just a few that can shift on any phase of the moon. Few years down the road, even your aunt Constance may get the gift. Hard to say, though. Nobody's figured out why some packs can and others can't. My big bro', Hector, was the first of us to get it. Light of the crescent moon burned smack dab into the middle of his forehead the first time. Lucky for the rest of us, the change happened a little less painfully."

"Well," Sunshine said. "That's pretty neat." She turned

to Death and Cooper. "By the way, this is Mr. Death and our new friend, Cooper."

Ike and Death gave each other a nod. "What's happening, old pal? You ready for one heck of a brawl?"

"You know each other?" Sunshine asked before Death could answer Ike. "Oh yeah. Ol' Grim goes way back with the pack. He'll never admit it, but they say he was on our side during the war."

Cooper scooted his chair forward. "Hey, um, Ike. About the war, I just want you to know I wasn't around for any of that. And if I was, I wouldn't have, well, you know."

Ike laughed and walked over to Cooper, patting him on the back. "Sounds like you figured you were on lil' Constance's bad side. Don't sweat it, kid. She'll come around. That was a real long time ago, and 'long as you're hanging out with us, you're with the good guys."

"What do you mean?" Sunshine asked, not sure what they were talking about. Before she could get an answer, a howl resonated through the halls of Darksmith Manor, coming from the West Tower. Ike's laid-back demeanor was instantly replaced with a snarl as his nose pointed in the direction of the baying wolf. "Pack it up, folks. Fear's on the march."

Chapter Eight

Fear Himself

Gathered in the courtyard with the others, Hector and Zeke, two of Ike's brothers, distributed weapons and gear to everyone. "Should be all you need," Hector said as he handed an iron club to Sunshine. The crescent-shaped scar on his forehead was just as Ike had described. "Any of those little buggers gets near you, just give 'em a knock in the noggin with this, and they'll be down for the count."

Sunshine frowned, looking at the crude device. "That doesn't seem very nice. Couldn't we just catch them in a cage, so I could talk to them later and just tell them to behave? I can do that, you know."

"I know, I know," Hector said. "Won't have enough time for all that, I reckon. But don't worry about that thing. It'll just put them in a daze, so after everything calms down, you can go do your Darksmith thing on them." Sunshine

accepted, figuring there are worse things that could be done than a mild clobbering. "That said," Hector started back up, "as for the bigger baddies, you leave them for the older folks. I'm not sure what sort of creeps Fear has working with him, but the big ones usually take more than a tap with an iron club." Sunshine saluted him and marched her way over to Constance.

"Hi, Auntie Constance," Sunshine said, skipping up to her aunt. Constance was in the process of strapping gear onto the back of Ike, who had now shape-shifted into a three-legged wolf.

"Hey, kiddo. You gonna ride with me out to Munstro?"

"Sure," Sunshine answered, climbing onto Ike's back. "I have a question, though. Once we get there, how are we gonna stop Mr. Fear?"

"Honestly," Constance said, her face overly calm, "I have no idea. We've never actually had the chance to get close enough to Fear to give him a run for his money. We've always gotten there too late, or he'd managed to sneak off too quickly. Since we've never had a true face-to-face with him, we don't know the best way to take him down. So, when we get to Munstro, when we find Fear, we're going to hit him with everything we've got. I figure he'll still be pretty fumed about the other day when we showed up, so I doubt he's got an escape plan all lined up. Right now, though, he's got his temper working against him."

Sunshine wrinkled her forehead in thought. "We aren't gonna kill him, are we?" Constance didn't have an answer for her.

"As it would be," Death intervened, "That may not be an option."

Constance and Sunshine looked to Death, not fully understanding what he meant. "When your father inherited Darksmith Manor, he set out to create the ultimate monster. Although each attempt outshined his previous achievement, Dominick continued to find disappointment. Until one day, he realized, it should not be the beast which drives the fear, but the fear which forms the beast. Once armed with that understanding, he exhausted countless resources from the Darksmith legacy to harness the pure terror necessary to create this monstrosity. Once perfected, Fear had not only been born to this world as the greatest of his kind, but also as an idea, unrestrained by his own mortality. I do wish I could give you an answer as to what we must do once we confront Fear, but I cannot. Although true defeat of Fear may not be possible, by drawing his attention away from the citizens of this world, we at least spare their lives. It is a risk, but we must take it."

"Hey, Sunshine," Cooper called out as he ran toward her and Constance. "Mum wanted you to take these with you." Cooper handed her a small, canvas sack.

Opening the sack and peeking in, Sunshine's eyes lit up. "Outsprouts! These'll be all sorts of good. Thanks!"

"No problemo," Cooper replied. "You guys be safe out there and have some fun."

Sunshine looked confused, "You're not coming?" Cooper shook his head, "Nah. Mum's got me and a couple of Ike's brothers staying behind to help out in case Fear shows up here before you guys get back. Says she always wished she had a Deadish here to help in the garden. Our type of folks got a special talent of talking to worms and grubbies, get 'em digging around where we want 'em to, and it's supposed to work the dirt up real nice. She said with me helping do that, she'll have her plants all set and this place ready to go in no time."

Sunshine seemed a little disappointed that her new friend was not riding into battle with them. "Oh. Well, that's good. Hey, check out my basher stick." Cooper's bloodshot eyes lit up as she twirled the club in the air.

Sunshine watched the ground speed by beneath them as she and Constance, riding Ike, raced to the Towne of Munstro. Ike, whose stride was surprisingly smooth despite only having three legs to run on, trailed closely behind his older brother, Hector. Hector, also having shifted to the form of a wolf, carried Doc, who was

trying desperately to keep from dropping the gadgets and tools he had brought to fend off Fear and his forces. Behind them, Bunny worked to keep pace with Zeke, occasionally running on all fours like a long-eared gorilla. From time to time, Death came into view, surrounded by swirls of black smoke as he levitated above the ground while racing alongside the others. Constance held tightly onto Sunshine as the group left the fields surrounding Darksmith Manor and entered the western forest.

Although it was still early in the afternoon, the branches that loomed over the old trail blocked out most of the light from the sun. Sunshine shifted around on Ike's back to get more comfortable as they slowed their pace to a more leisurely trot. Looking back at Constance, Sunshine whispered, "Auntie Constance, are you scared?"

Constance, who was still holding onto Sunshine, loosened her grip. "No, Sunshine. Not really. I've been mixed up in stuff like this for a while now. Long enough to know when to stay gutsy. What about you? Are you okay?"

Sunshine looked around at the trees as she thought about the question for a moment. "Yeah. I don't think I'm scared. We're the good guys, after all."

"Yeah, we are."

Sunshine, still hanging tight to Ike's fur, turned her head to face Constance. "How come you don't like Cooper?"

Constance sighed, debating how to explain. "It's nothing personal, but ... well ... You know a long time ago there was a war, the War of Fang and Fur, right?"

Sunshine nodded, "Yep. Mr. Death told me that's when he met my great-great-great grandpa."

"Yeah. Well, that war was between werewolves, like me and Ike and his brothers, against vampires."

Sunshine looked surprised, "Vampires! I didn't know ..." Then realizing all she had been seeing lately, said, "Oh. I guess that makes sense. But how come everybody was fighting?"

"The war started because the vampires wanted to lock up all the people in the world, and werewolves, well, we're not the kind of folks that take kindly to things like that. Back then, there were lots more of us. We did what we could to help out the regular folks. The vampires were outnumbered and, needing to level the playing field, started recruiting. The easiest way for them to do that was to go after the Deadish, like your friend, Cooper."

Sunshine frowned, "But Cooper would never team up with the bad guys."

"That's just it, though. Even if the Deadish had chosen not to side with them, it wouldn't have mattered. Those no good, disco-dancing blood suckers can control them, make them fight on their side whether the Deadish want to or not. Even if it's someone you trust with your life, if a vampire wants them, the Deadish are powerless to stop it."

Sunshine turned back around, sad to think that her friend could be helpless against a vampire. The forest seemed too quiet as they continued toward the Towne of Munstro. Sunshine noticed Hector, who had a long lead, stop in his tracks. Ike, Zeke, and Constance also seemed to be alerted by something. As they all stood in silence, Sunshine looked back and forth between the trees and bushes, trying to find what had caught the attention of the werewolves. Realizing she had been searching with the wrong sense, Sunshine cringed as the stench hit her nose. "Oh, gross!"

A long, quiet spell was shattered by the thunder of trees being crushed and toppled. Constance leapt down from Ike's back as the wolves braced for attack.

"Same one as before?" Hector growled.

"Yep, same one," Ike said, baring his jagged teeth.

As the noise flooded the path, Sunshine squeezed the handle of her club, not sure what was coming. All of a sudden, branches exploded outward as a sasquatch, the same that had ripped the arm off Bunny, jumped through the air. The snapping jaws of the wolves narrowly missed their target as it hurdled over them. The beast leapt and grabbed onto one of the lower branches of a tree, still staying out of reach of the wolves. Its free arm reached out, pointing a colossal hand directly at Sunshine. Before she could react, the beast threw a small branch, which landed right in front of her on Ike's back. And then, for some reason, Sunshine didn't feel Ike beneath her. In fact, she didn't feel anything at all.

The forest above her parted to reveal the sky. Rainbows, twirling around the sun, danced with clouds as raindrops floated like little, crystal orbs. She reached out and touched the sun, rolling it around the ceiling of the sky. Then, taking hold of the blazing ball, she threw it as far as she could, far beyond the horizon. The world went dark, but soon, dusk began to reverse itself, and the sun came back to her, this time being carried by a mountainous wolf. Sunshine climbed up the paw of the creature and watched its jaws open to release the sun. As the sun's flames curled off it, the giant ball floated back to its place, now becoming the moon. The wolf looked up at it and howled. Again and again it howled until Sunshine began howling with it. Then, she realized what the wolf was saying in its howls and listened closely as it called out her name, "Sunshine."

As the familiar stench of the sasquatch filled her nose, Sunshine found herself curled up on the ground. Trying to sit up, she looked at Constance, "What happened?"

Constance helped her to her feet. "I think you might be

allergic to clothoberries."

"Clothoberries? Where did we ...?" Sunshine shrieked as she saw the sasquatch slowly approach Bunny. "It's Bigfoot! Bunny, behind you!"

Constance patted Sunshine on the head. "It's okay. The sasquatch is here to help." Sunshine watched in disbelief as the mangy monster handed a bundle of abnormally large carrots to Bunny. Constance held a large bag up to Sunshine, "It looks like she figured out who you were and wanted to do some good. Brought a whole bushel of clothoberries to give you."

Sunshine, now even more in shock, "Really? That's great ... Did you say 'she'?"

Constance smiled, "Yep. I think her name is Bray. Sasquatch can talk something close to wolf-speak, but the accent's a bit thick, so it's hard to say exactly."

Sunshine crept over to Bunny and the sasquatch, trying not to gag. "Hi ... Bray. Thanks for the clothoberries ... and the carrots." Bray grunted as she smiled, which let out even more of the stink causing Sunshine to flinch. "Welcome to the team."

After passing through the forest, they entered a wide

field. Sunshine recognized the field from when she and Constance had first left the Towne of Munstro on their way to find Mum. Off in the distance, she saw billows of smoke rising from the town.

"Hurry, everyone," Hector yelled as he erupted into a full sprint toward Munstro. Constance held Sunshine tightly as Ike leapt over the tall grass. Bunny and Bray moved forward to cover the flanks on each side as Zeke raced to catch up with Hector. Death, who was drifting swiftly beside Ike, disappeared in a cloud of black smoke.

Bouncing up and down on Ike's back, Sunshine noticed Doc at the front of the group. Fumbling with his instruments, he barely managed to stay seated on Hector. He began attaching the loose instruments to the pack on his back. Soon, Sunshine realized each attachment jutting out from the pack was part of a weapon, making Doc look like a peacock of war. Just as he completed his device, they arrived at the gates of the Towne of Munstro.

Chaos filled the streets while people ran by carrying pitchforks, torches, and various tools to defend the town from its attackers. Sunshine clenched her iron club as she watched wicked creatures spring from roof to roof. Menacing shadows that seemed to come from nowhere floated across the walls of buildings. Gangs of little gremlins, possibly relatives of Hiccup, scurried by, tearing down anything their tiny arms could reach.

"Get to the town hall," Hector ordered the others. "That's where the mayor will be organizing the villagers."

They headed deeper into the town and found more creatures vandalizing the homes and small stores that lined the streets. Sunshine saw a blur rushing toward Zeke.

"Look out, Zeke!" she yelled. Just in time, Zeke spotted the creature. Though hardly standing taller than Sunshine, a tiny minotaur charged with the force of a full-sized bull. Zeke grabbed it in his jaws. Spinning around, he flung the beast through the wall of a teashop. Glasses and dishes shattered as shelves and tables collapsed, burying the minotaur in debris.

"Leave it," Doc said as he jumped down from Hector's back. "We're almost there." Doc pulled a cord on his pack, and two robotic legs shot out. Now carried by the chicken-like legs, Doc dangled in the air. Taking control of them, he darted off toward the center of town.

At the town hall, they found a mob of villagers already engaged in battle with Fear's minions. Wielding a huge spear, Felix Dragulus, the mayor of the Towne of Munstro, stood at the top of the stairs leading into the town hall. He swung his weapon at the creatures crawling toward him. As he knocked them back, he spotted Sunshine and the others.

Constance pulled Sunshine down from Ike as the others

headed into the melee. Bunny and Bray held back the various fiends as the werewolves made their way to the villagers.

"Stay close," Constance told Sunshine as they moved through the crowd. Suddenly, a creature with the face of a vulture lashed out at Sunshine. Without hesitation, she whacked it on top of the head with her club.

"Sorry," Sunshine said, cringing as the creature thudded against the ground.

"Where is he?" Constance yelled to Mayor Felix as they reached him. "Where's Fear?"

The mayor, now being protected by a few of the villagers, wrestled his staff out of the grip of a scaled tentacle. "I haven't seen him, not yet," he answered.

Sunshine looked beyond the town hall's steps to the pandemonium of the courtyard. It looked as though the town had been swallowed by a nightmare as the motley legion of monsters overwhelmed the townspeople.

Down one of the cobblestone streets leading to the town hall, Sunshine saw a dark figure emerging from a flurry of smoke. "Death!" she yelled. However, she quickly realized a flood of vile creatures was chasing him. "Constance," she pointed at Death. "We have to help!"

Constance smirked, sheathing her weapon. "He'll be fine."

"But there's so many," Sunshine trembled. "They're almost right on top of him."

"No," Constance smiled. "They're with him. Those are the Strays."

Constance watched the Strays battle their way closer to the mayhem in the town square. As Death approached, Fear's fiends turned away from the villagers and began lunging at the Strays. Fur and feathers flew as giant jaws chomped slime-covered skin. Creatures breathing fire were met by water that seemed to be alive. A group of tiny minotaurs collided with the even smaller, armored gnomes. Sunshine felt a hand land on her shoulder. She looked up to see the mayor. "Quickly, get inside."

Sunshine and Constance followed him into the town hall while Doc, Bunny, Bray, and the werewolves fought off the horde. The mayor led them to a map of the Towne of Munstro in the large, empty meeting room. "They first attacked coming through both the cemetery and by the northern road," he said, pointing at the map.

"Where else have they attacked already?" Constance asked. "We're going after Fear, and I doubt he'll still be hanging around areas that have already been destroyed." The mayor began pointing at places around the map, showing Constance where Fear's minions had already struck.

Sunshine noticed someone enter the room. "Hello, Sunshine Saliente," the young boy greeted her.

"Yetzel," Sunshine said, quickly remembering the nastiness of this seemingly pleasant child.

"I'm glad you're here," Yetzel said as he looked out the window, disturbingly unaffected by the events happening outside. "After we met, I did a bit of research. It is somewhat rare that a new face arrives in the Towne of Munstro. That, along with the haunting familiarity of the name Saliente, I found to be quite intriguing."

Yetzel pulled a paper from his jacket pocket and unrolled it, ignoring a stream of blue jelly spraying across the window behind him. Holding up the old document, he read aloud, "For the forbidden offense of the use of the black arts within the borders of the Great Towne of Munstro, I, Mayor Felix Dragulus, set forth my decree. Flora Adora, previously unknown to be a practitioner of witchcraft, let show her wicked ways to result in the death of not only a citizen of the Great Towne of Munstro, but of our most revered Master Hunter, protector of our people, defender of our lands. Let it be known that on this day, the foreigner Salvo Saliente, resident of Shwibala and accomplice in this most heinous act of villainy, and Flora Adora, are, forevermore, ensured by blade and ancient rite, exiled from the Great Towne of Munstro."

Sunshine, perplexed by what she had just heard, looked at Yetzel, "What is that? Momsy never killed anybody."

Yetzel rolled the paper and slid it back into his jacket. "Oh, I have my doubts that she did. After all, 'to result in the death' seems a tad elusive on the part of my father. What I find truly interesting here are the ancient rites of exile."

Yetzel walked over to the window and held his head high, looking past the muck on the glass and beyond the battle below the building. "These old enchantments, set in place long before the old war, still hold strong potency. Did you know that once banishment from the Towne of Munstro has befallen a person, it is absolutely and physically impossible for them to return? And not just to the town itself, but even as distant as St. Lucky's. Furthermore, the banishment applies to generation after generation of the exiled's descendants."

"What's your point?" Sunshine asked, suspicious of where he was headed with this.

"My point," he said softly, "is that I know exactly who you are."

"Come on, Sunshine," Constance said, taking her by the arm. "We've got an idea where we can find Fear."

Sunshine stared back at Yetzel as Constance pulled her out of the meeting room.

The mayor led Constance and Sunshine out of the town hall. The villagers, with the aid of Sunshine's companions and the Strays, seemed to have made some headway against the invading ghouls. Mayor Felix worked his way through the mob of villagers. "Everyone!" he shouted. "To the cemetery!"

Constance and Sunshine ran up behind Ike. "We're going to work our way to the southern docks and then back along the seawall. We should be able to force Fear out and have him surrounded by the north dock. Once we've got his attention, we push him east, heading back toward Darksmith."

Sunshine stayed between the werewolves, bopping any critter that got too close for comfort. Doc, Bunny, and Bray held up the rear, pushing them forward. Just before reaching the docks, they faced a wall of monsters blocking the path. Sunshine, peeking past the legs of her entourage, saw a puddle of water at the feet of Fear's minions.

"I've got it!" Sunshine shouted to everyone. She pulled out the outsprouts Cooper had given her and launched them into the puddle. Instantly, the little plants went to work. The green outsprout unleashed a noxious belch as the red one snapped at their enemies' heels. The yellow outsprout sucked up the puddle, filling itself until it couldn't take in another drop. The water blasted any of the creatures that had managed to stay standing through the foul cloud left by the green outsprout and knocked them back.

Just past the dazed monsters, the harbor came into view. Sunshine saw they hadn't yet had a chance to repair any of the seaside buildings destroyed by the tidal wave caused by the Leviathan. At last, they reached the southern docks. They stopped in their tracks as shrieking laughter rang throughout the air.

"This is it!" Constance yelled. "That's Fear!"

As his name left her lips, flames erupted from the ground. Doc quickly grabbed one of the attachments on his backpack and aimed it at the fire. Pulling the trigger, thick foam blasted and drowned the inferno.

"He must be close," Doc said, his metallic, chicken-leg suit stepping over the steaming foam. "Start heading toward the north dock.

Anxiously, they searched for Fear. Darkness suddenly blanketed the town. Black clouds filled the sky as lightning flashed, and the wind began to howl. Sunshine readied her club, waiting for something to pop out at her. But before anything could, Fear's taunting laughter sounded once again. Sunshine's eyes traveled up the cathedral and

saw a dark silhouette clinging to its spire. The creature leapt down, cackling all the way. Its hoofed feet shattered the stone ground where it landed.

"Mr. Fear," Sunshine whispered to herself. She watched the fire burn in his eyes beneath his wide-brimmed, pointed hat. Sunshine was transfixed by the jagged grin that was carved into his pumpkin face.

"What are you mutts doing here?" Fear screamed, pointing his slimy, wart-covered hand at Hector. "Who are you to interfere?"

Hector stepped forward, snarling at Fear. "You've no right to be here. Call off your fiends, or we'll tear you apart."

"Ah, ah, ah, little doggy," Fear said, waving his finger at him. "Munstro is mine for the taking. When I'm through, this world will be nothing but my brethren, true acolytes of evil. I'm only sorry you've chosen the wrong side." Fear raised his hands into the air. "Now, watch helplessly as my minions destroy the humans that plague our land!"

Fear's army came into view near the north dock, running toward their master. Closely behind them were the villagers, led by Mayor Felix and the Strays. Fear hissed as he saw his army being chased down.

"This is it, Fear," Hector growled. "This is the end." Fear took hold of his weapon, a broken bone ground into a blade, and prepared to attack.

"Not the best idea," said a soft voice from the shadows. "The odds are against you in this fight. May be in your best interest to change targets."

Sunshine peeked around Ike to see what was happening. Her eyes quivered as she saw the small boy appear from the darkness, and she croaked, "Yetzel."

"What are you doing, kid?" Hector barked. "Get back!"

Yetzel walked out from the shadows, heading straight for Fear. The commotion came to a pause. The Strays, the villagers, and Fear's monsters all watched as the boy walked toward certain doom.

"I know what you are," Yetzel said, looking at Fear. "The embodiment of all the anxieties of humankind rolled into one foul creature. However, what I am afraid of is not you. What I am afraid of is the thought that the affliction that has burdened my home for generation after generation may one day return. The very cause of the problems we are facing now."

He looked back at the villagers and the mayor. "For ages, my father and those before him overlooked the abominations that have plagued our land. And now, as you, Fear, attack the Great Towne of Munstro, you fail to realize you stand before your true goal. In front of you is Sunshine Saliente, daughter of Dominick and Delilah Darksmith and heiress to Darksmith Manor."

The crowd froze. Fear looked at Yetzel and then to the wolves. Sunshine squeezed her club as their eyes met. Finally, he had found the child he had hunted for since her birth. Fear burst into vicious laughter.

"Little sister," Fear grinned. "Sunshine Saliente. A happy little name for a Darksmith. I gave up on meeting you. Gave up on taking what should be mine, the power of Darksmith Manor, the power to create the greatest evil imaginable and bring proper chaos back to this world."

Fear turned to Yetzel, "You did the right thing, kid. You'll make one heck of a mayor." His arm swung into Yetzel, launching him into the wall of the cathedral. Fear lunged toward the villagers, then, leaping into the air, snapped his wide jaws shut around the head of Mayor Felix Dragulus. Yetzel, only dazed for a moment, looked up to see his father's headless body fall to the ground.

Leaping back up to the spire of the cathedral, Fear yelled, "Troops, fall back!" Sunshine stared at him as he pointed down to her, "By sunrise, Darksmith Manor will be mine." Fear disappeared into the darkness while his minions below trampled their way out of the Towne of Munstro.

Chapter Nine

The Madness

Death appeared in front of Sunshine as the villagers carried away the body of their mayor. "Sunshine," Death said, walking beside her. "As I brought Mayor Felix to the great beyond, he asked that I warn you to be wary of his son."

"No kidding," Sunshine said, trying to see where Yetzel had gone. "He didn't even look like he cared after …" Sunshine kicked at the ground, her stomach churning at the memory. "Let's just get back home. The plan's ruined anyhow. If we hurry, maybe I can try to make those skellies again."

"Very well," Death agreed. "The Strays are already on their way."

Sunshine turned toward Ike, ready to hop on and leave

the Towne of Munstro. As she gripped a handful of hair, she noticed something coming in their direction. By the north dock, dozens of Fear's minions marched toward their group … their now highly outnumbered group. They all braced for another battle, but then, Sunshine felt as though something were different.

"Wait," she yelled, as she ran in front of the werewolves. Staring at the approaching fiends, she walked forward until the small army came to a stop. A froggish little creature placed his long spear on the ground and hopped up to Sunshine.

The frog-like creature snorted and stared a bit at Sunshine as she stared back at him. Pulling off his hat, a moldy lily pad from the top of his head, he let out a croak. "It true?" his garbled voice managed to ask, "You the Darksmith girl?"

Sunshine smiled and nodded. She pulled the medallion from her shirt and showed him. He stopped breathing as he recognized the symbol. The frog-man fell to his knees, bowing to Sunshine. As he did, all the beasts behind him did, as well.

Sunshine looked in disbelief at the army before her. She kneeled down to the slimy creature. "Hey," she whispered. "What's your name?"

Still bowing, he peeked up with one eye. "Frokki," he

grunted. "At service for you."

"Okay." Sunshine leaned in closer. "Frokki, we're going back to Darksmith Manor. Could you be in charge of leading all your buddies up there for me?"

Frokki picked up his spear and stood up as tall as he could. Lifting it above his head, he cheered, "We do good! We Darksmith!"

With that, all the beasts behind him stood and cheered. "We Darksmith," they chanted.

Frokki jumped onto the back of a furry, yet slug-bodied creature. "We Darksmith! We gonna fix up. No more Fear! He bad guy. We good guy! We Darksmith!" Frokki jumped down again. "Come on, everybody!" Frokki hopped down the road, leading the massive army past Sunshine.

She watched and waved to all of them. "See you there. Thanks for the help!" Monsters of all shapes and sizes marched by. Even with their vicious fangs filling their gaping mouths, they seemed to smile upon seeing the return of the heiress of Darksmith Manor.

Sunshine walked between Death and Constance on their way out of the Towne of Munstro. Ike and Hector had both returned to their human forms as they led the way with Doc, Bunny, and Bray. In the distance, Sunshine could hear the townspeople gathering.

"I'm sad for the people," Sunshine said, looking toward the sound of the commotion. "The mayor wasn't very nice to us, but they seemed to like him a lot."

Constance patted her on the head. "I'm sorry you had to see that happen. I didn't think Fear would've attacked him, but now the people are going to be scared with no one to lead them."

Sunshine shuffled her feet as she walked. "How come Yetzel told Fear that I'm a Darksmith? We could have stopped him back there, and then the mayor would be okay."

"He was just trying to get Fear off his people's backs," Constance told her. "It's what we would have eventually done. He just threw off the timing."

"He's mean," Sunshine said unhappily. "He told me Momsy got banished because she got somebody killed. That's not true, right?"

"Definitely not," Constance assured her. "The man he was referring to was the Master Hunter of the Towne of Munstro. Back in those days, the mayor had started hunting down stray monsters from Darksmith Manor, ones that had run off or ones that their owners didn't

want to take care of anymore. The man he had hired was
Therion Deathberry, your uncle."

"My uncle?"

"Yup. Long story short, he was working with Salvo, your
Pop, at the time. They were trying to take down a pretty
savage beastie, and your Momsy showed up just in time.
She saved Pop. Didn't have a chance to help Therion,
but you can bet your behind she tried to. Delilah never
blamed her for that. It was the mayor. Therion was his
golden boy, the solution to his Darksmith problem. That's
why he forced her to leave."

"But Yetzel said she did witchcraft, too. Is Momsy a
witch?"

Constance chuckled, "No, not really. Flora and Delilah
used to play around in the dark arts, but nothing too
serious. I think Delilah did it just to impress Dominick,
and well, let's just say it was a good thing your Momsy
knew some tricks, because she was able to keep Pop from
getting hurt."

Sunshine sighed, "It's too bad Pop and Momsy can't come
stay with us. I really miss them."

Constance took Sunshine's hand, "Maybe someday."

Darksmith Manor appeared just over a distant hill in the surrounding field. Sunshine ran ahead of the group toward her new home. As she reached the top of the hill, her eyes widened. Below her, hundreds of monsters surrounded the manor.

"Hurry! Let's go see everyone," Sunshine shouted to Constance and the others.

When they reached the army, growls and grunts greeted them. Sunshine smiled, waving and saying hello to all the hideous new faces. She recognized some of the creatures from earlier, but most were new. Flocks of winged, lion-headed women circled above as lizard men in wooden masks delivered buckets of dirt to a hungry golem, each bite causing it to grow in size. The minotaurs who had defected from Fear's army now played cards and traded weapons with the gnomes who they had recently battled.

"There you finally are," Mum Furley called as Cooper chased after her. "You must have brought in half of Fear's army. And the Strays, too? I have no idea how we'll ever be able to accommodate all of our guests."

"It won't be long," said Hector, who looked much older as a human than he did as a wolf. "Fear claimed to be attempting to take Darksmith Manor by sunrise. Despite how despicable he is, he's always kept to his threats."

"Sunrise?" Mum said. "The evening's hardly even begun. We may have to wait up all night before he shows."

"But maybe not," Hector replied. "Everyone should stay alert. Let's use the questionable time we have now to do whatever we can. Sunshine, you may be young, but this is your army. It's up to you to decide what to do."

Sunshine didn't respond, staring in silence at the crowd of creatures she had never before imagined. She pictured each one of these beasts being created at the hands of her forefathers and seemed to feel a hint of what they must have in each of their accomplishments. "Sunshine," Hector said softly.

She turned around. A grin stretched across her face, and a mad sparkle glinted in her eye. "Let's make my skellies."

Doc, Mum, Cooper, and Constance tried to keep pace with Sunshine as she ran through the halls of Darksmith Manor. She jumped onto the rail of the spiral basement stairs and slid all the way down. She ran to the twirligig, the skeletons still dangling from their spiderweb shackles.

"I couldn't find anything wrong with the setup," Doc said as Sunshine circled the machine, poking and prodding at random parts.

"There isn't anything wrong with it," Sunshine responded. "It was me. I wasn't Darksmith enough."

Cooper moved in closer, trying to figure out what she was doing. "You weren't Darksmith enough?"

"Nope," she answered. "It's what Death told me about. About the Madness. You can't just have all the right stuff. You've gotta feel it."

Doc scowled, "The Madness. That old myth has nothing to do with making monsters. Science is what you need, munchkin. The right ingredients, proper engineering, and plenty of research."

"Nope," Sunshine disagreed. "I've got a whole army of creatures at my doorstep. That's all I need." A toothy grin stretched across her little face as she pulled the start-up crank. The twirligig erupted into a spin, even faster than before. Sunshine climbed up the stepladder to the operating table and grabbed the two hoses that she had used to bring life to the bat wing and Snippersnap. Holding them both under one arm, she twisted their handles, blasting bolts of electricity and ectoplasmic goo into the twirligig. Doc, Mum, Cooper, and Constance watched in shock as the little girl burst into maniacal laughter.

Doc leaned over to Mum, "She's just like her father."

The Madness

"I know," Mum whispered back. "I'm so proud."

Finally slowing to a stop, the twirligig's structure began to bend and snap. Cables from the control panel whipped around violently, snapping off the machine. Sunshine grabbed the disconnected cables and plugged them back together. As she did, smoke spewed out from the machine. Hissing and crackling sparks filled the air. Then, those sounds were replaced by a chatter, a chatter of teeth clinking together.

"My skellies!" Sunshine cheered, the crazy look still in her eyes. "It worked!"

The skeletons all awoke together, trying to shake free from their bindings. Sunshine jumped down from the table and rushed over to them. "Welcome back to life, everybody!"

Constance ran to her side. "Be careful," she warned Sunshine. "They might not listen to you. Once upon a time, they were alive. Some of those old memories might still be there."

Sunshine, still overwhelmed with joy, reached into her shirt and pulled out her medallion. Holding it up to the skeletons, she yelled, "I'm Sunshine Saliente, the heiress to Darksmith Manor. I need your help to stop Mr. Fear and bring back the good old days for monsters everywhere!"

The skeletons seemed to calm down, no longer trying

to break out of the webbing. From the other side of the twirligig, the sound of bones rattling began.

"Did she say monsters?" the skeleton in the back asked anyone who would answer.

"I … I think she did," one on the side replied.

Sunshine, now confused, looked at the now trembling skeleton in front of her. He nervously looked back at her and then at Doc, Mum, and Constance. Then … then, he saw Cooper.

The skeleton let out a wail, "Zombie!" All the skeletons began panicking, shaking in their webbed shackles. The skeleton in the front turned to face the one to his right. He let out another scream, "Skeleton man!"

Sunshine walked back to Doc and the others. "They're kind of scaredy cats, huh?"

Doc stepped around Sunshine and up to the front skeleton. He put his hands on his hips and glared into the skull's empty eye sockets. "Now, listen here," he barked. "You are dead. Yep. Dead. Each and every one of you. At some point during your life you had all signed over your bodies to science upon your demise. Well, your demise has come and gone, and here you are. So, buck up folks and welcome back."

The front skeleton hung his head in disbelief. "I … I don't remember that. I don't really remember much of anything, not even my name."

Sunshine ran up in front of him. "It's okay. You can have a new name. A whole new life, too. We have a little emergency, and I'm hoping you guys can help."

"Cooper," the skeleton mumbled.

Cooper looked up, startled. "Did he just …"

"I like that name," the skeleton said. "My name could be Cooper."

Sunshine cringed a bit. "Oh, sorry. That name's already spoken for." She pointed her head toward Cooper.

"Oh, too bad," the skeleton said, looking as disappointed as a skeleton could. Then, his head shot up. "What about Elvis?" he asked excitedly. "I don't know why, but I like it!"

Sunshine thought about it for just a second and nodded. "Elvis it is. Now, let's get you guys down from there.

After the skeletons were off the twirligig, and the shock of being not much more than walking bones had faded away, Elvis walked up to Sunshine. "Thank you, I suppose. It's not quite what I expected the afterlife to be, but I'm happy to give it a try."

"Thanks," Sunshine grinned. "I'm glad you guys are here."

"Yes, yes. Though, earlier you said you had something you needed our help with. What do you need us to do?"

"Well," Sunshine started, then took a deep breath. "There's a bad guy on his way that's named Mr. Fear. He's a monster that was made here at Darksmith Manor by my dad a real long time ago, and he's really scary. He's the scariest, I guess, but I don't know for sure because I've only been here a few days. I haven't really met all the monsters there are to meet, so I don't know if Mr. Fear is really the scariest, but that's what people tell me, so I suppose he is. Anyway, he tried to take over Darksmith Manor a long time ago, but he couldn't because I was going to inherit it. So, when I was born he tried to eat me, which is real bad and gross, and I suppose maybe because of that, he is the scariest monster I ever met because nobody else has tried to eat me. But he didn't get to eat me because my dad stopped him, but both my parents died, so Auntie Constance and some other friends took me away to live with Pop and Momsy. Mr. Fear didn't know that, and he thought I was still here, and I guess he was still hungry and trying to get me, so for a real long time he was trying to get into Darksmith Manor. But when my dad died, he made a big, shiny force field thing around it, so Mr. Fear couldn't get inside to find me, even though I wasn't here, anyway. I guess he got bored trying to get in and went and found a bunch of other monsters, and they all started causing trouble. So, Auntie Constance and Mr. Death came and got me from Pop and Momsy so that I could take over Darksmith Manor so that Mr. Fear would leave people alone. But, now I'm back, and he knows that, so he's going to come and try to take over Darksmith Manor again ... and probably try to eat me."

Elvis stood frozen for a while, trying to sort out all of Sunshine's rapid ramblings. His bony head tilted as though everything had just made sense. Then, standing up proudly, Elvis raised his fist, "If protection from this menace is what you need, we will provide. For the gift of a second life, we skeletons will serve as your personal guard."

"We'll do what?" one of the other skeletons asked, his head poking out from behind the twirligig.

"Awesome," Sunshine smiled. "I'll call you the Boneyguards! Elvis and the Boneyguards. Ha! You guys should start a band."

"We're starting a band?" the skeleton behind the twirligig asked, now completely puzzled.

Sunshine and the others led the Boneyguards to the West Tower to prepare them for battle. When they arrived, they found Hector, Bunny, and Bray already there, along with a few others.

"Hi, everybody," Sunshine said, smiling. "Bunny, this is Elvis and the Boneyguards. They're the skeletons from the Purgatorium. They're gonna be our bodyguards. Since you kind of were that for me already, you get to be their boss. Elvis can be your second-in-command. That sounds good, right?" Bunny nodded happily, giving her two big, blue thumbs-up.

"What about me?" Cooper asked, his arms full of various weapons for the Boneyguards. "Since we're going to war, I should have some kind of cool title, don't you think?"

"Yep," Sunshine said. "I figured that all out on the way up from the lab. You and Ike and his brothers and Bray and Auntie Constance are officially the Knights of Darksmith. Hector and Death are my generals, and so is Frokki. You didn't meet him yet, but he's going to be in charge of everyone that used to be on Mr. Fear's side. Mum and Doc don't really need titles because they already have jobs for Darksmith."

Cooper grinned his decaying smile at Sunshine. "That's so cool! I'm a Knight of Darksmith!" He handed the rest of the equipment to the skeletons, keeping a small hatchet for himself. "What'll be my first order, m'lady?"

Sunshine laughed, surprised at Cooper's eagerness. "Hmm. Why don't you find General Frokki and have him meet us in the big dining hall, so we can figure out a plan?"

"Aye, aye," Cooper answered, then bolted out of the room.

Constance looked up from a conversation she was having with two people Sunshine hadn't yet met. "Rounding up the troops, kiddo?"

"Yep. I don't really know what I'm doing, so I'm just doing what feels natural."

"Good girl," Constance said, walking over to Sunshine. She pointed over to the two men she had been talking with. Both were wearing headbands with the same moon symbol Ike had on his. The taller man had long, black hair in thin dreadlocks, while the shorter man had a bushy handlebar mustache surrounding his jolly smile. "That's Skip, the tall one is Lloyd. A couple more of Ike's brothers."

"Really," Sunshine squinted. "Brothers of Ike keep popping up. I should let them know I just made them Knights of Darksmith."

"Yeah. So I heard. You don't really need to, though. Most of the people, monsters, ghouls, and what have you that are here have been loyal to the Darksmith name for a long time. Heck, once this is all over, you'll probably have trouble getting rid of some of them."

Sunshine's eyes lit up. "That would be great! There are all sorts of extra bedrooms here."

"You, young lady, have never cleaned up after a house full of monsters."

Sunshine, walking with Bunny and being followed by her Boneyguards, saw Doc heading to the grand hall, pushing a chalkboard. She thought she heard him muttering something under his breath each time the loose wheel pulled the board into the wall.

"Hello, Doctor Bratenlager," she said as she skipped up behind him. "Need some help?"

"What? Oh. No, no. Just a stupid wheel. Keeps dragging the thing off course."

"Bunny," Sunshine yelled back. "Would you mind?"

Bunny caught up with them and picked up the chalkboard with one hand. Sunshine gave him a grin as he carried it off to the hall to meet with everyone else.

"Sooo ..." Sunshine started, holding her flowered pen and a sheet of paper to take notes on. "Any ideas on what we're going to do once Mr. Fear shows up? We've got lots of people here, but what if we have to do something special, like a stake through the heart or zap him with a laser or make him eat Pop's pine needle stew?"

Doc looked at Sunshine, "Pop's what?"

"Pine needle stew," Sunshine said, her nose wrinkled. "It was real gross."

"Oh," Doc shrugged. "Well, nothing figured out yet. Went through some old notes and couldn't track down any way to 'once and for all' him. That's how Dominick and I made him. Had to be as scary as possible, so what's worse than a whole lotta evil that you can't even stop?"

"Even I still have no solution." Doc and Sunshine turned as Death approached them from the adjoining hallway. "After reviewing millennia of my work, nothing compares to a fiend such as Fear."

Sunshine perked up, "What if we can capture him? We could lock him up in the dungeon. Maybe we could talk him out of being such a baddie."

"Nope," Doc said, shaking his head. "I had set a good lot of traps all 'round the manor after it was sealed up. Sure as I figured, Fear was back here trying to claw his way in and set off every one of them. Not one held him, though. Your old man really did make the monster of monsters when he came up with Fear. Used to always have some sort of failsafe for the things we'd conjure up, but ol' Dominick thought it would ruin the 'integrity' of his masterpiece."

"What about Nocnitia," Sunshine asked, looking at Death. "Couldn't you send him there without his dying?"

Death pondered the idea for a moment then shook his head. "Nocnitia, the realm of nightmares and resting place for the souls of monsters, is unlike that of humans. The borders of the human afterlife can vary, at times wavering into thin spots. This is what allows memories of the deceased to remain strong and, occasionally, permits the comings and goings of spirits and the like. The boundaries of Nocnitia, however, are ironclad. These are spirits of things that were never meant to be, and as such, their souls must be bound to that place as tightly as they can to prevent any prohibited travel. Therefore, he must be dead to enter."

Sunshine looked woefully at Death. "What if we can't beat him? What if he does eat me? What if he eats me, and then he takes over Darksmith Manor, and everybody has to work for him doing bad stuff that they don't want to do?"

Death knelt down beside Sunshine. "Sunshine Saliente, you are a Darksmith. I have watched closely over the work of the last five generations of your family. In that time, I

have witnessed the most unexpected solutions to the most
unanticipated situations. Be it by the Madness your kin
have some unparalleled access to, or simply a knack for
seeing light in times of darkness, they by and large prevail.
I do not foresee your fate waiting in the grasp of Fear. You
have much to do here. Much to do, indeed. Darksmith
Manor will rise again to the glory it has once known, and
by your hand, it shall be done."

"Well," Sunshine shrugged. "I guess we'll figure it out
when we need to figure it out. Now let's hurry to the big
hall, so we can run this army!"

As Sunshine, Death, and Doc entered the grand hall,
torches along the walls filled the room with light .The
night sky gazed in through the ceiling-high windows.
Bunny was rolling the chalkboard back and forth, trying
to find a good place to put it. Sunshine saw Constance at
a table with Ike, Hector, and the other brothers. Mum was
in the back, trimming old, dried up leaves off Buckley's
branches. As she tended to the short, timeworn tree,
Venaticus darted back and forth between the legs of the
long, wooden table she sat at. Just behind Sunshine, Elvis
and the Boneyguards arrived in the room, quickly looking
around to ensure that everything was secure.

Doc ran over to Bunny, showed him where to set up the
chalkboard, and began drawing a picture of Darksmith

Manor, surrounded by little X's and O's to represent the vast army of creatures that filled the outlying field. Death motioned his bony hand to Sunshine, leading her to the table at the head of the room. She climbed onto the chair at the center of the table and stood on it to see the leaders of her army.

"I don't see Cooper or General Frokki yet," she whispered back to Death.

Death looked over the room, "Cooper is probably still trying to find him."

"Bummer," Sunshine said. "I think I should give a big, important, really motivating speech to everybody to get them all ready to go to stop Mr. Fear. I should probably wait for them, though."

Doc walked over to the other side of the table, in front of Sunshine. "I've got the preliminary plans all drawn up, so if you want to get things started, go right ahead."

Sunshine shrugged, "We're still waiting for Cooper to find Frokki and bring him here. General Frokki is in charge of a whole lot of the folks that worked for Mr. Fear, so he should be here for this."

Just then, Cooper crashed into the room. Everyone's head spun around to see what had happened. Cooper looked startled, and as soon as he was about to speak someone yelled, "Zombie!" The Boneyguards all charged him.

"Wait!" Sunshine shouted. "That's Cooper! He's on our side."

"Oops," Elvis said as he skidded to a stop. "Sorry, pal. Just got to be on guard. It's our job."

Cooper shook it off, still with the panicked look he had when first crashing into the grand hall. His arm swung behind him, pointing back through the door, "We're under attack."

Chapter Ten

Heiress of Darksmith

Everyone rushed after Sunshine who raced out the front doors of Darksmith Manor. The intensity of the growls and grunts of her army grew as an orange glow crawled closer, coming from the western woods. Bunny picked Sunshine up, trying to give her a view above her army of monsters.

"It's too far," she shouted. "I can't see what's coming. I can't tell how many there are." She looked around, trying to find a better vantage point. Then, she spotted the massive telescope protruding out of the roof of the West Tower. "There! I need to get up there!"

Bunny ran as fast as he could, carrying Sunshine to the wall of the tower. She looked around trying to find a quick way to get all the way up. "We can't climb up. The vines are all cut down ... Wait! That's it!" Sunshine looked toward the front of Darksmith Manor, still covered in a few vines. "The Snippersnap! He's still working." She hopped down from Bunny's arms and ran toward the vines. Bunny, Constance, and Cooper chased after her.

Finally finding one of her first creations, she yelled out, "Snippersnap! I need your help!" The bat-winged shears fluttered down, snipping at the air on the way. "I need you to carry me up there," she said, pointing at the giant telescope. The Snippersnap closed its blades, allowing Sunshine to grab on.

"What are you doing," Constance yelled. "You know it isn't safe to fly with scissors."

"It'll be okay," Sunshine said. "He's one of mine."

The Snippersnap took off, carrying Sunshine to the top of the tower wall. They reached the roof and flew into the outer access, just below the telescope. Sunshine jumped to the floor of the room and ran to the eyepiece. She looked through it, seeing the Towne of Munstro as if it were right next door.

"We need to move this thing," Sunshine yelled to the Snippersnap as it flapped its wings mindlessly. Sunshine examined the device, trying to determine which lever did what. Not finding any rhyme or reason to how the machine worked, she began pulling whichever lever her hands landed on. The telescope swung left and right, up

and down, still not finding Fear and his army, not allowing Sunshine to see what they were up against. Finally, it fell right into place. Sunshine's jaw dropped as the bloodthirsty faces filled the eyepiece.

The Snippersnap followed after her as she ran to the opening in the roof. She leaned over and, spotting Constance and the others below, yelled down, "It isn't Mr. Fear! It's Yetzel! He's leading a bunch of people from Munstro."

Constance put her hands to her mouth and shouted back, "How many are there? How many are coming?"

"I'm not sure," Sunshine replied, straining her voice. "A hundred, I think." She grabbed the Snippersnap. "Let's go back down there," she told it.

As she landed, Constance ran up to her. "If Yetzel has come here looking for a fight," Constance growled, "he'll be getting a lot more than an angry mob can handle. Sunshine, call back the Strays and Fear's old monsters. Hector and I will try to calm down the villagers. Once you have the monsters all in place, rush up to the front line with Doc, Mum, and anyone else, so we can work out a quick truce with the people of Munstro."

"Why are they doing this? Why are they angry at us?" Sunshine asked her aunt.

Constance smiled at her, "This used to happen all
the time. The villagers get mad about something the
Darksmiths have done, they gather up their torches and
pitchforks, and send out the mob. But, if we let them try
to take on all of these monsters, it won't be pretty, kiddo.
It really won't be pretty."

Sunshine nodded, "Okay. Let's go."

Constance headed toward the oncoming villagers, letting
out the best howl she could with her human body to
summon Hector, Ike, and their brothers.

Sunshine turned to see Cooper, Doc, Mum, Bunny,
and Death, all awaiting her orders. "You heard Auntie
Constance. Let's get all these critters back by Darksmith
Manor, so they don't start fighting. We need to be on the
lookout for Mr. Fear. He's the real bad guy."

They all gave a quick nod and headed out in separate
directions, while Death vanished in a swirl of black smoke.
Sunshine watched for a moment as the smoky vapor
seemed to hang in the air. She reached out to touch it. As
her fingers came in contact with the misty darkness, they
felt cold, then, they felt as though they were no longer
attached to her body. She pulled her hand back and
looked at it. She wiggled her fingers, happy to see that
they were all still there. She quickly shook off the strange
sensation as she turned to run to the front of the crowd.

"Head back to the house, everybody," she yelled as she ran past the battle-ready beasts. "That's not Mr. Fear up there! We're not gonna fight them." Though hesitant, the mangy monsters and creepy creatures turned back. When she reached the frontline, she ran back and forth, jumping up and down. "Everybody go back to Darksmith Manor and wait for Mr. Fear. These are the people from Munstro. We don't want to fight them. They're our pals!" Slowly, but surely, the horde withdrew.

Sunshine saw Doc and Cooper nearby and hurried over to them. "They're going back," Cooper told Sunshine as they met each other. "I found Frokki. He's leading them away from the villagers."

"Good," Sunshine said, trying to catch her breath. "Let's go talk to the villagers and get them to leave before Mr. Fear shows up."

Mum and Bunny reached Sunshine and the others on the way to meet Yetzel. Constance was there with Ike and all of his brothers, staring down the angry mob from fifty feet away. The brothers all looked ready to transform into their beastly forms at a moment's notice.

"Your father never would have done this, Yetzel," Constance yelled. "Call off the townspeople before somebody gets hurt."

Yetzel shook his torch at her, embers exploding in the

air. "My father never would have done this because he couldn't see the source of the problem. Fear wouldn't be here, if not for the vile witchcraft and blasphemous acts of Darksmith Manor. He tried to maintain balance with you fiends, but no more. I, Yetzel Dragulus, am now mayor of the Great Towne of Munstro and will not allow Darksmith Manor to stand yet another day." The villagers cheered, raising their torches and pitchforks.

"Stop!" Sunshine shouted. "None of us need to fight. I like the Towne of Munstro, and I don't want any of the monsters to be bad to you. All these monsters, all these hundreds of monsters are here because they don't want to cause trouble with you. They're here to stop Mr. Fear, to make up for what's happened."

Sunshine walked halfway between Constance and Yetzel. "Just give me a chance. Once Mr. Fear is gone, I can get all the monsters that have been lost and scared back on track. I never even knew there was a place like this in the whole world, and now I'm here and have all sorts of great friends. We can all live in peace. We can all work together."

Yetzel stared at Sunshine, his teeth clenched. His hand beneath his cloak slowly reached for his dagger. But before he could pull it from its sheath, the ground began to tremble.

Ike and the rest of the brothers twisted to the north, transforming instantly as they each dropped to their

clawed paws. Hector let out a howl as Constance pulled out the long, silvery spike she always carried with her.

"The girl's right," one of the shopkeepers from Munstro hollered. "Things were good enough for me when the Duke was around." He pointed to the north, toward the Howling Mountains as the earth continued to shake. "That's our real problem."

Creatures charged toward them by land and sky. Sunshine watched beasts and ghouls that couldn't possibly be real coming straight for her. Though their numbers were no more than the army waiting at Darksmith Manor, these abominations made up for it in nastiness. Hideous beasts, taller than the towers of Darksmith Manor, were followed by a scourge of monsters brandishing crooked blades and weapons that might even cause injuries just by looking at them.

"Everyone," Sunshine yelled. "Get back to the house." She turned to Yetzel and the villagers, pulling out her small, iron club. "Stay with us or go back to Munstro. We're going to stop Fear whether you help us or not."

Sunshine turned and ran toward Bunny. She looked back and saw everyone from Munstro running with her, ready to join the werewolves, monsters, and other creatures that they had been prepared to fight moments ago. Everyone but Yetzel. Glaring at Sunshine, he stood still as the villagers sped around him.

"This isn't over, Sunshine Saliente," he screamed over the stomping mob. "Even if you stop Fear tonight, I will still be here to bring down Darksmith Manor tomorrow!" Yetzel turned his back on the cheering villagers and slipped into the darkness of the night.

Sunshine clung to Bunny's head and shoulders, and they hurried through the fields surrounding Darksmith Manor. The pack of werewolves ran alongside them as their human and formerly human companions followed behind.

"Hurry," Elvis yelled to the Boneyguards. "We must protect the Lady of Darksmith!" The newly armored skeletons flung themselves forward to keep up with the giant, blue rabbit as he made his way past the army of monsters.

"Mr. Fear is here," Sunshine yelled to her army. She spotted Frokki hopping toward her. "General Frokki, protect Darksmith Manor. Don't let them get by you!"

"We do good, boss," he belched. "We Darksmith!"

Sunshine reached the door with Bunny, followed quickly by Elvis and the Boneyguards, Ike, Hector and their brothers, Constance, Doc, Mum, and Cooper. Out of a surge of black smoke, Death emerged to join them once again. The villagers arrived just behind, their faces stricken with terror as they saw the ghoulish army in which they had volunteered to serve.

From Bunny's shoulders, Sunshine turned to everyone. "This is it. It's time to stop Mr. Fear. I don't know how we'll do it, but we have to. We can't be afraid of Fear. Doc, Mr. Death, Mum … you all worked for Darksmith Manor when my parents were alive. I've seen some of the amazing things you've created. Together, we can figure out how to stop him. Hector, Ike … I need you to make sure we have enough time to figure it out. Make sure he doesn't get through. The villagers will help you, too."

She turned to the people of Munstro. "Don't be afraid. We're all in this together. Those monsters with Mr. Fear might be coming here to destroy us all, but we can stop them. We can stand up to the bad guys and bring back peace between Darksmith Manor and the great Towne of Munstro. Once we end this fighting, you can all sleep tight because giant, bloodthirsty, face-eating bedbugs won't bite." The villagers looked at each other, still with looks of worry. But then, seeing a tiny, little girl standing in the middle of werewolves, monster-makers, and other things that should not be, they raised their torches and pitchforks and cheered victoriously.

Sunshine climbed down and took the furry hand of Bunny and the rotting hand of Cooper. "You guys are my team. I couldn't have made it this far without you.

Now, it's time to end this and see what comes next." She turned to Elvis and the Boneyguards. "You guys are just awesome."

She looked at Constance and quickly ran up and hugged her. "Auntie Constance, thank you so much for bringing me here. Even if Mr. Fear does eat me tonight, this has still been the best adventure me and Bunny have been on. I want you to stay with me until this is all over."

Constance hugged Sunshine tightly. "Of course I will. Now let's win this fight."

Elvis and the Boneyguards circled the lab, making sure everything was secure. Doc unrolled blueprints across his operating table. Sunshine, Cooper, Mum, Bunny, Death, and Constance all looked down at the original design for Fear.

"If we're going to find a way to snuff out Fear," Doc said, "this is where we start."

Death stepped back from the table. "As we have explained before, Fear, as he was created, has no vulnerabilities."

Sunshine studied the sketch, her eyes squinting thoughtfully at the hand drawn jack-o'-lantern face staring back at her. "What if … what if we could go after the parts he was made from? Like the ingredients? If, maybe, we just took out a single thing, it might make him weaker."

Mum leaned in for a closer look. "Hellfire," she said to herself. She looked up at Doc. "She may be on to something. It says here that Hellfire was one of the components in Fear's creation. Back when you first used Hellfire, you nearly burned down your lab, but we managed to put it out. If we could counteract it …"

Doc shook his head. "I thought we agreed to never bring up that incident? Regardless, it won't work. Jester's Tears is what we used on the Hellfire flames. And see, right there." He pointed at the list of elements used to create Fear. "Jester's Tears. Part of the reason he enjoys what he does as much as he does. For everything we used to make this wretch, we threw in the remedy. He's like rock, paper, scissors, all rolled up into one."

They all stood in silence for a moment, going over the various ideas running through each of their heads. Sunshine held her hand to her chin as she thought, looking down at the floor. A droplet splattered just where her eyes had been gazing. She looked up at the light-green liquid's source.

Cooper noticed Sunshine watching him as he scratched at one of the festering boils on his arm. "Oh, sorry," he said, embarrassed. "They swell up a bit when I'm nervous."

"Eureka!" Sunshine shouted, leaping toward the small puddle of puss on the floor. "Doc! Cooper's skin goo! When I got close to the clothoberries, you used it to make me better. There aren't any clothoberries or Deadish ooze in Mr. Fear."

Doc looked intrigued for only a second, but then waved his finger in the air. "If neither one was used to make him, then if we threw just one at him, it would have nothing to counteract. And either one on its own wouldn't do much of anything to Fear."

"That's why we add one of them to him," Sunshine said with a mad grin stretching across her little face. "We add Cooper's slime juice to him like it's a whole new ingredient, but a whole lot so it's super important inside him. Then, we blast him with clothoberries. Or, we do the clothoberries first. Either way, it'll work."

Everyone looked at Doc, then at Sunshine, then back at Doc, waiting to see his response. Doc smiled at Sunshine as the mad glare twinkled in her eyes, "That's the look I was waiting for. Let's do it. We'll set a trap. However, if we add clothoberries to Fear first, we have the problem of your allergies kicking up. We'll suck out some of Cooper's guck and set the machine up with that. Then, we hit him with the berry juice. We have to act fast. I don't know what'll happen once Fear gets loaded up with necro-goo. He could become even more dangerous."

Sunshine clapped happily, "Ha! Bunny, you and Doc and Mum and Cooper, bring the twirligig down to the dungeon and set everything up. Crazy Legs can help us, too. He can sticky-web Mr. Fear to the twirligig. Me and Auntie Constance and Mr. Death will lead him down there. Make sure the elevator's back up so we can get back to you quick. When we get down there, have it all ready."

Sunshine ran to the spiral stairs, surrounded by the Boneyguards. Death slid up beside her. "Hurry, Sunshine. I'll meet you on the battlegrounds. My post as Reaper beckons me."

The Boneyguards burst through the entrance of Darksmith Manor, Sunshine and Constance close behind. "Stay close," Constance told Sunshine, her weapon in hand. "As soon as we spot Fear, let him see us, then start running back."

They ran through the battle as the two armies of monsters clashed. The Boneyguards formed a circle around Sunshine and Constance, trying to protect them from the lashing talons and snapping jaws. Sunshine hopped up and down, desperately looking for any sign of Fear.

"There's Ike," Constance yelled to Elvis. "Get us over there. I'm sure that's where we'll find Fear."

Just then, a screech wailed above them, and Sunshine looked up to see a dragon with two, massive, bat-like wings. She grinned in awe, hoping this was one of her allies. As they reached Ike, the rest of his brothers were there with him, all in wolf form.

"Where's Fear?" Constance yelled to Ike.

Ike quickly tossed a goblin from the grasp of his teeth and looked back at her. "There," his muzzle turned, and both Constance and Sunshine looked to see where it pointed.

Fear stood, perched on the shoulder of a giant, cackling as he watched the mayhem below him. Sunshine moved to the edge of the circle of Boneyguards, looking for some way to get his attention. Then, she could feel the answer burning in her chest … or rather, *on* her chest. She reached into her shirt and grabbed the Darksmith pendant. The medallion was warm, the skull-shaped crest glowing a hot white. She held it up in Fear's direction and yelled, "Mr. Fear! I am Sunshine Saliente, and Darksmith Manor belongs to me!"

White flames shot out of the pendant, blasting into Fear's gut and sending him tumbling from the giant's shoulder. Sunshine looked at the pendant, shocked by what it had just done. Soon though, she saw Fear rise to his feet.

"Little sister," he hissed. "Tonight, I'm going to finish what I started so many Halloweens ago. Tonight, my belly

will be full, and all these beasts will bow before Fear."

Constance grabbed Sunshine's arm. "Run."

As they ran back toward Darksmith Manor, Constance scooped Sunshine up and rushed past the Boneyguards. "Elvis, try to slow him down. She'll be fine with me." The skeletons halted, ready to sacrifice themselves to keep their maker safe.

Constance set Sunshine down as they reached the door. "Hurry, get inside!"

Sunshine pulled the door open and quickly looked back as the battle behind them continued to rage on. She spotted Elvis and the Boneyguards just as Fear reached them. She stared in disbelief, watching bones explode into the air, Fear bowling through them unhindered.

"Oh no," Sunshine said in a whimper, slipping through the door.

"Don't worry," Constance reassured her. "We can put them back together later. Let's just get downstairs for now."

Sunshine and Constance arrived in the laboratory only to find the scuff marks on the floor from where Bunny had pushed the twirligig back to the elevator. A black cloud of smoke appeared in front of them. Death emerged as the vapor sifted through the air.

"My apologies for not being able to help out there," he said, leading them to the elevator. "War keeps me fairly occupied."

"It's okay, Mr. Death," Sunshine told him. "But we have to hurry now. I think Mr. Fear is inside."

Shrill laughter echoed through Darksmith Manor, letting her know she was right. They all rushed to the elevator door, Constance pulling on the candlestick to open the secret entrance. The bricks began to move apart to reveal the elevator door. Then, they stopped.

"What in the – " Constance jerked at the candlestick. The bricks shook, trying to open further but still only gave a gap that even Sunshine couldn't fit through.

"Hurry," Sunshine said, tugging at Constance's dress.

"I'm trying. The door's jammed!" Constance pulled on the bricks, attempting to open it by hand.

"Constance," Death said quietly. "He's here."

A shadow stretched across the wall leading down from the spiral stairs. Fear's hideous laughter filled the lab as

Sunshine, Constance, and Death stood there helplessly. Then, a pointed hat followed by a rotting pumpkin face came into view. Fear stood at the top of the stairs, staring at Sunshine.

Death stepped forward. He held out his skeletal hand, and black smoke swirled around his palm and between his white fingers. From the smoke, Death's scythe emerged in his hand. "Protect the girl and find a way in. I shall handle Fear."

Fear crept down the stairs, still staring at Sunshine. "For so long, I clawed at the seal that I thought was keeping you safe. If only I had known I would have just needed to lay waste to a few villages to draw you out, I would have done it years ago. But here we are. Here we are, and there's nothing you can do to stop me."

Death held up his scythe. "We will see about that." He vanished in a swirl of mist. In an instant, Death stood in front of Fear, the scythe already swinging at the snarling pumpkin face. Fear dodged. He leapt from the stairs, crashing into Death and sending them both flying. Death disappeared once again, reappearing behind Fear. Fear jumped to his hoofed feet, laughing as he stabbed his sharp bone knife at Death. Death blocked Fear's blade with the staff of his scythe, knocking Fear back. Fear slammed against the operating table. Death stood in front of him, staring down. Darkness filled the air.

"The sands of time may not hold sway over the abomination that you have become," Death bellowed, "but the pain of death I may still deliver." He raised his hand to Fear's grimacing face. One finger stretched out, touching Fear between the eyes.

Fear screamed in pain. Death struggled to stay in contact. The effort of trying to take the life from that which could not be killed used all of his strength. Death's touch released, and they both fell to their knees. Then, Fear looked up to Death, his maniacal laugh beginning once again.

"That was incredible," Fear cackled. "But as much fun as we're having, I've really got more important things to do." Fear lifted the operating table. Raising it high above his head, he hissed, "So long, Grim." Fear slammed the metal table down, smashing it into Death. Black plumes of smoke billowed out from the crash.

"Death!" Constance screamed. She lunged at Fear, her silvery spike swinging down toward his face.

Fear looked up, the stake was just inches from his eye. Before it could pierce the rotting jack-o'-lantern face, the ground below him gave way. One of his hoofed feet fell through the crumbling floor, saving him from Constance's weapon. He steadied himself and grabbed her, his clawed hands wrapping around her head.

"You missed," Fear grinned, then tossed her across the room. Constance flew into the wall and fell to the floor.

Fear pulled his leg from the hole as the floor of the lab continued to crumble into the dungeon below. He lurched toward Sunshine. "Now, where were we?" Fear crept closer. "Oh, that's right. Dinner time."

Sunshine backed up into the bricks that hid the elevator, gripping her club. Fear moved closer and closer, drool pouring from between his jagged, orange teeth. Sunshine swung the iron club, striking Fear in the side of the head. Fear stopped.

"Really?" He looked at her, appalled. "Did you really think that could possibly stop the inevitable?" He burst into laughter.

Sunshine stood tall as Fear continued to mock her. "No. I just needed to distract you."

Fear regained his crooked composure. "Distract me? Distract me from what?"

Sunshine smiled, then pointed toward the corner of the lab. Fear turned to see Constance hunched over and staring at him, her yellow eyes glowing. Her teeth gritted against each other as a deep growl grew from behind them. Her shoulders jerked as fur jetted out of her skin. Claws emerged from her slender fingers, and all the muscles in her body twitched and reshaped, changing her into her hidden form. Constance hurled herself at Fear, catching his shoulder in her vicious jaws. They tumbled backward, rolling to the center of the laboratory. The crumbling floor gave way, opening a gaping hole just where they had landed. Fear and Constance fell into the dungeon, disappearing into the darkness.

Sunshine ran to the hole, trying to see through the pitch-black emptiness. "Well," she said to herself. "Here goes nothing." Sunshine jumped, flapping her arms, not knowing when the ground would find her.

The landing was gentler than she had expected as she hit the floor and rolled to her side. She searched through the dim torchlight in the dungeon to see what had broken her fall. Fear lay there, twitching. Sunshine jumped to her feet.

"Auntie Constance," she whispered. "Where are you?"

"Right here," the voice came from the darkness. Constance emerged, panting, yet no longer in her wolf form. "I've never done that before, changed without the moon. It's pretty rough, kiddo."

"You were awesome!" Sunshine cheered. "Let's hurry and find the others before he gets up."
They ran through the corridor, past the cells and toward

the main room of the dungeon. "Is Mr. Death okay, do you think?" Sunshine asked as they ran.

"I don't know," Constance said, brushing dust off her shoulders. "I hope so. I'm sure he is."

Doc spotted the girls as they entered the Purgatorium. "Everything's just about ready. What was going on up there?"

Sunshine hurried over to him. "Your lab kind of got broke. Mr. Fear's here. He's in the dungeon."

"Hurry along, then," Doc told them. "Cooper's been trying to get your pal, Crazy Legs, over here, but he's half unconscious after getting all that necro-goo pumped out of him. Find them so you can get your spider set to blast Fear into the twirligig."

"Okay," Sunshine said. She started to run off, but one foot was frozen in place. A tight squeeze seemed to overcome her leg and as she looked down, she saw the reason why. A clawed, wart-covered hand clung to her ankle. Sunshine screamed, trying to shake free from Fear's grip. Just as she screamed, Fear let go.

She watched in astonishment as he went flying toward the ceiling, whipping back and forth, from one wall to the other. Then she saw what looked like green tentacles thrashing through the air.

"Take that, dirt bag!" Mum Furley shouted from across the room, holding a small pot. Sunshine realized the tentacles were vines springing out of the pot.

Sunshine ran past the twirligig and saw Cooper clinging to the back of Crazy Legs. "Cooper, Crazy Legs," she shouted. "Over here! Mr. Fear is here!"

Cooper did his best to steer the giant spider down to Sunshine. Crazy Legs scurried toward Sunshine, then, suddenly leapt into the air, right at her. Sunshine let out a quick scream and hid her head under her arms. She felt a tug at her back, and the floor below her disappeared.

She opened her eyes to see one of the spider's legs flicking at Fear, who must have broken free from Mum's vines and returned for the attack on Sunshine. She looked up to see Bunny holding her upside down, high out of danger. She crawled up his arm, finding a seat on his shoulder. Bunny held her in place with one arm and with the other grabbed Fear. He flung Fear against the twirligig.

"Now!" Sunshine yelled to Crazy Legs. "Stick him to it!"

Crazy Legs sprayed his webbing, covering Fear and pinning him to the carousel of doom. Sunshine jumped down from Bunny's shoulder, rushed to the control panel and pulled the lever as hard as she could. She burst out laughing, more menacingly than Fear himself.

The machine spun in a blinding whirl. Sunshine slammed her fist into a button, releasing the necro-goo that Doc had harvested from Cooper. Light and smoke were sent in all directions from the twirligig. The canister of green fluid drained, and Fear was flung from the machine, crashing against the dungeon wall and falling to the floor.

Sunshine ran to the smoky cloud. Then, a screech wailed through the Purgatorium.

Fear rose from the clearing smoke, fire burning behind his jagged face. His body convulsed as this new component coursed through his veins. "I can feel it, the blood of the dead." He cackled as his body became more and more twisted, evolving him into something even more vile. "This power ... is incredible! Now, I will finish you once and for all. You stupid ... little ... people."

Fear raised his hand, and the twirligig rose with it. Still spinning, the machine flew toward the wall. Gripping it and crawling across the wall, the twirligig circled furiously. The occupants of the Purgatorium were now trapped in the center of a tornado.

Fear staggered toward Sunshine as she backed toward the middle of the room. "And now, little sister, Darksmith Manor is mine!" He sprang toward her, his jaws spread wide enough to swallow her whole.

"Sunshine!" Doc yelled. "Hold your breath!" He threw a massive syringe to her.

Just in time, she caught it. The syringe was filled with glowing, white liquid. She held it out with her eyes closed. She could feel the force of Fear crashing into her. As she cautiously peeked at him, Fear's face hung right in front of hers. Sunshine looked at him, still holding her breath, and then forced herself back, leaving the syringe lodged in his chest.

Fear shook as the medley of life and death battled inside him. Flames spewed out from his pumpkin face as he hissed. Then, as the internal conflict left no victor, Fear's body sank to the ground.

Everyone ran to Sunshine as she watched Fear lie motionless in front of her.

Constance put her hand on Sunshine's head. "You did it, kiddo. It's over."

Sunshine started to smile, but before she could, she let out a scream. Fear was back up, lunging at her, the sharpened bone he used to kill her father, flying at her face.

Then, all that she could see was blue. "No," she muttered as her giant, furry friend slumped to the floor. "Bunny!"

Fear jumped over Bunny and grabbed Sunshine, his

pumpkin face raving mad. Still, Sunshine just stared at Bunny, her closest companion for as long as she could remember, lying there, after only recently having been given the gift of life. A black cloud swirled around the giant rabbit. Death had returned, this time to claim her friend.

"I am sorry, Sunshine," Death whispered, just before vanishing once again in the swirl of darkness.

Then, snapping back to what was happening, Sunshine looked Fear in the face. Her courage came back to her, along with the same feeling she had when she first created the Snippersnap. She could remember the sound of the chattering teeth as the boneyguards came to life. She could feel the Madness, the same feeling her father, Dominick Darksmith, must have felt when he brought Fear into this world.

Her little face twitched as a warped grin stretched from ear to ear. Sunshine shoved him with all the strength she could gather, taking Fear by surprise. She drove him backward into the black smoke that took her friend, her first creation, away.

Sunshine could feel icy cold rushing through her hands, then nothing. Fear could feel it, too. The chill, filling his deformed body, forcing a scream from his wicked soul. Sunshine pulled away from him, falling backward. The smoke engulfed Fear, tearing him apart as he struggled,

taking him against his will into the afterlife.

And then, Fear was no more.

Everyone watched in silence as the smoke cleared.
Sunshine stood up and saw that there, where Fear had
just been ripped from this world and into Nocnitia, rested
something small. She walked over to it and picked it up. It
was Bunny, just as he had been before she had ever known
anything about Darksmith Manor or the fate that had
been waiting for her. She turned him over and pushed the
cotton fluff back into the hole that now scarred his chest.

Sunshine turned back to the others to find herself facing
Death's dark cloak. She looked up to see his skeletal face
looking down at her. "It worked, Sunshine. Fear now rests
in Nocnitia and will be bound there forever."

Sunshine stared at him sadly, hugging Bunny. Death knelt
down to her. "Your friend is fine. His sacrifice, his death,
may not be able to be undone, but even with this, you
carry part of him with you."

Sunshine sighed and looked at her stuffed rabbit,
remembering all the adventures they had even before their
ride with Captain Moby aboard the Typhoonicane. She
smiled at Death. "When you see him, thank him for me ...
for us."

"I will," Death said. "For now, we should find the others."

Sunshine and the others walked through the doors of Darksmith Manor, discovering that all the fighting had stopped. Ike, Hector, and their brothers stood waiting for them. Sitting on top of Bray's head like a living hat, Frokki held up his webbed hands in victory. As Sunshine approached her army, they all cheered together.

Frokki leapt down from his perch atop Bray and hopped over to Sunshine. "You beat Fear! You beat Fear, and everybody stop fighting! We win! We Darksmith!"

Sunshine giggled, "Yeah. No more Mr. Fear. Everything can be back to normal now."

Hector and Ike, along with some of the villagers from the Towne of Munstro, approached her. "After you defeated Fear," Hector, now in his human form, said, "his army must have known it. They backed down immediately and started helping their wounded. However, there'll still be work to patch up some of the bad blood that Fear's attacks caused. The townspeople will do what they can to keep him in check, but young Yetzel's running the show over there."

"I think it'll be okay," Sunshine said, nodding. "We did all this by working together. If we keep it up, things will be great!"

Frokki happily bounced up and down. "Ha ha! We Darksmith. We do good! What now?"

Sunshine looked at him. "What now? What do you mean?

Frokki slowed down his hopping, letting out a belch. "No more Fear. Lots of creepy crawlies, no job. Nothing to do. Nowhere to go."

Sunshine looked out at the hundreds of monsters, all without a purpose in the world. She looked back at Doc, Mum, and the others. "Well," she said, wondering. Then, a mad grin stretched across her face, "Everybody can stay here!"

The monsters around them growled, grunted, hissed, slurped, and wailed in a cheer as Doc Bratenlager's head fell into his hands. Mum Furley simply let out an exhausted sigh.

Epilogue

Dear Pop and Momsy,

I miss you guys so much. Things at Darksmith Manor are great. Everybody is awesome. There's a lot I have to do, though. It's been a real long time since any of these monsters had someone to take care of them. I want to start learning how to make monsters, but first, I'm going to help the ones that are here and get things back on track.

I really want to see you soon, so I'll try to figure out how. I know you can't come here, but from what I've seen lately, anything can happen.

Big hugs and kisses,

Sunshine

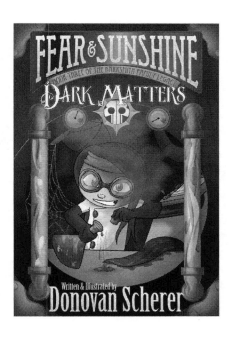

Other Books by Donovan Scherer

You can find an up to date list of all my books at:

www.DonovanScherer.com/MyBooks

For the Teachers and the Students

If you would like to test the nuggets of knowledge
that this book has slipped into your brain
or are looking for resources for your classroom,
please visit:

www.DonovanScherer.com/Resources

... but if you just want to zone out and color some pictures,
here you go:

www.BreakfastDoodles.com/LetsColor

Think post-apocalyptic Alice in Wonderland with robots...

Lost Tomorrow is yours for free.

Before her journey to the world of Darksmith Manor, Sunshine Saliente had plenty of adventures with her stuffed rabbit, Bunny. *Lost Tomorrow* brings our dear little heiress of madness to a post-apocalyptic wonderland where the few survivors will do anything to make sure she has the best time of her life, whether she wants to or not.

You can get a free ebook copy of Lost Tomorrow when you sign up for my newsletter. Along with that book, you'll get a handful of other stories, some weird goodies, and news for whatever is next.

Visit www.DonovanScherer.com/Newsletter/
to get your free ebook

About the Author

I'm Donovan Scherer, an author and illustrator creating worlds of adventure with a sense of humor and a little bit of dread that everything will go terribly, terribly wrong. I tend to think in cartoon, but since animation would take me longer than I'd like to keep you waiting on my stories, I write and illustrate them instead.

You can find all the places I'm at online at:

www.DonovanScherer.com/Online

Made in the USA
San Bernardino, CA
06 October 2016